.

TIME BETWEEN TRAINS

ALSO BY ANTHONY BUKOSKI

Twelve Below Zero

Children of Strangers

Polonaise

TIME
BETWEEN
TRAINS

Stories by Anthony Bukoski

Southern Methodist University Press
Dallas

Copyright © 2003 by Anthony Bukoski
First edition, 2003
All rights reserved

Requests for permission to reproduce material from this work should be sent to:
Rights and Permissions
Southern Methodist University Press
PO Box 750415
Dallas, Texas 75275-0415

Grateful acknowledgment is made for permission to quote from "Revolt in Verse," by Bogdan Czaykowski. Used by permission of the author.

The stories in this collection first appeared in the following publications: "A Geography of Snow" and "Leokadia and Fireflies" in *Chronicles: A Magazine of American Culture*; "Time Between Trains" in *Louisiana Literature: A Review of Literature and the Humanities*, Southeastern Louisiana University, Hammond, Louisiana; "Holy Walker" as "March of Dimes" in *Passages North*; "Leaves That Shimmer in the Slightest Breeze" as "True Adventures" in *Twelve Below Zero* (New Rivers Press); "The Moon of the Grass Fires" in *Wisconsin Academy Review*; and "It Had To Be You" as "A Balcony Story" in *Alabama Literary Review*. "A Philosophy of Dust" appeared as "The Waiter Michael Zimski" in *New Orleans Review*; "The Value of Numbers" in *Between Stone and Flesh*, a Holy Cow! Press anthology; and "President of the Past" in *To Be: 2B*.

Cover art: Ben Shahn, *Scotts Run, West Virginia*, 1937. Tempera on cardboard, 22¼ × 27⅞ in., collection of Whitney Museum of American Art, 38.11. Copyright © Estate of Ben Shahn/Licensed by VAGA, New York, NY.

Jacket and text design: David Timmons

LIBRARY OF CONGRESS CATALOGING-IN-PUBLICATION DATA

Bukoski, Anthony.
  Time between trains : stories / by Anthony Bukoski.—1st ed.
    p. cm.
  ISBN 0-87074-479-8 (alk. paper)
  1. Wisconsin—Social life and customs—Fiction. 2. Polish Americans—Fiction. I. Title.
PS3552.U399T56 2003
813'.54—dc21

                                    2003042719

Printed in the United States of America on acid-free paper
10   9   8   7   6   5   4   3   2

For my cousin Joe Novack,
with Abiding Affection

Acknowledgments

I AM DEEPLY GRATEFUL, once more, to Kathryn Lang, my editor, who has guided me through three books. For their generosity, I am indebted to the University of Wisconsin–Superior Foundation and to Charles Schelin, former provost/vice chancellor, who encouraged faculty research and publication during his tenure at our school. I am also thankful for the support given me by LaMoine and Mary Ellen MacLaughlin of the Northern Lakes Center for the Arts, Amery, Wisconsin, and for the boundless goodwill of my friends Timothy Crow and Barton Sutter. Finally, without my wife Elaine's patience and understanding, this book could not have been written.

I was born there.
I did not choose the place.
Why was I not born simply in the grass.
Grass grows everywhere.

BOGDAN CZAYKOWSKI, "Revolt in Verse"

Contents

A Geography of Snow

MY FATHER has to go out in a storm. An eight-hour shift at the gasworks, then two or three hours tomorrow morning, All Saints' Day morning, in a bar where Happy Hour starts at seven-thirty in the morning and ends at noon, and home through the snow he'll walk, stinking of beer and CH_4, the chemical composition of natural gas. If you want to know how it smells in our house, scratch and sniff the card the utility company gives you so you can detect a leak in your gas-burning appliances. What the company adds is an "odorant." My father and our house smell like an odorant.

Pani—or "Madam"—Pilsudski, our neighbor, likes the smell when she comes over. "Oo-la-la," she says when she gets a whiff. As my father grumbles and I page through my scrapbook of interesting newspaper articles, Mother starts talking to her in Polish in the living room. Having important things to do on my hobby, I try not to listen.

My scrapbook has a three-ring metal binding and gray canvas covers. In light blue ink, I'm writing on the front cover, "STRANGE, FUNNY NEWS GATHERED BY ANDREW BORUCZKI." The cover is hard to write on, and I have to go over the letters, almost carving them in. The front cover looks sloppy, which, when he sees it, serves as an irritant, not an odorant, to my father, who is trying to raise me right and who, sitting here in a sleeveless undershirt with a tuft of hair curling up from his chest, says to me, "What're you doing?"

"Studying my newspaper clippings."

"Why you won't think of me for one minute? I gotta go out in this weather to the plant. Put the scrapbook away and ask, 'What can I do for my father?'"

When I do ask, he answers, "I don't know. Just don't bury your head in a scrapbook all a-time."

In five hours, he has to leave for work on a night the radio said would be clear and mild. The weather depresses him. His job, combined with his naturally gloomy personality, inspire him to get drunk at the Warsaw Tavern, especially now around All Saints' Day. When the weather and your job stink, when your life is passing you by and you will soon be a dead soul yourself, why not go on a rumba? To relieve the pressures of my life, I can't go to taverns like he does; but tonight, if he doesn't stop complaining, I'll do something drastic and tomorrow's newspaper will read, "Adolescent punches gas-stinking father during blizzard," which will replace the lead clipping in my collection. In my scrapbook, the current No. 1 Best Story, Pick of the Week from the *Superior Evening Telegram* of October 25–31, 1968, tells of a woman who ties her boy's hands together, dresses him in a pig suit, then puts him on public display. It is from California, an Associated Press story. As further punishment, the mother hangs a sign on her boy in the pig suit. The sign reads:

> I'm dumb pig [sic]. Ugly is what you will become if you
> lie and steal. Look at me squeel [sic]. My hands are tied
> because I cannot be trusted. This is a lesson to be
> learned. Look. Laugh. Thief. Stealing. Bad bo [sic].

"MOM DENIES ABUSING SON DRESSED AS PIG," says the headline. (I had to look up what "*sic*" means.)

Another clipping reports on something closer to home. You will find it on page 2 of my binder under the title "Child Abuse":

Gerard Lenahan, Gordon, Wisc., used a marker to write
"liar" in large letters on his ten-year-old son's forehead,
"I lied to friends and teacher" on his chest, and "I tell
stories" on his back. Then he took his shirtless son to
P&R Pub in Hawthorne and made him talk to customers and display the writings.

Now my pop mutters, "They promised a sunny day and look-it what we got!"

He uses the Polish word for snow, *śnieg*. Four or five inches of it cover the birdbath.

"Maybe this'll be my last Halloween to go trick or treating," I say. "And who's going to give out candy on a stormy night like this?"

"I *geev* candy," Mrs. Pilsudski says.

"Boy's too old for trick or treating," my pop says. "What're you, nineteen?"

"Fourteen. Tad's nineteen," I say referring to my cousin. Home from Vietnam, he is named after Thaddeus Kosciuszko, the Polish patriot who helped General Washington win the Revolution.

"Ah, go upstairs," says Pa. "Read your scrapbook. Play with your winter weed collection. Look at the weather. No, lemme tell you a thing or two. You know what's falling outside?"

"What?" I ask as I leave the kitchen.

"Shit from the sky."

"*Sheet* from sky," Mrs. Pilsudski says in her broken English.

"That's northern Wisconsin for you," Pa says. "Worst climate in the world is in 'Siberior,'" a word he's made up combining "Superior" and "Siberia."

In the living room, I watch Ma and Mrs. Pilsudski, who whispers, "*Sheet* from sky," over and over as she stares out at the weather. Ma says we must be patient with Mrs. Pilsudski when she forgets and leaves open the bathroom door at our house, but I saw what she was doing once and it was awful. She wore heavy black shoes, thick, skin-colored stockings, and a shapeless house-dress with yellow cornstalks on it, a style of dress a lot of Old Country women around here wear. Girdle about her knees, the heavyset Mrs. Pilsudski, who cuts the calluses off of people's feet for a living, hovered over our toilet. Through the open door, I spotted her busying herself, and I cannot say more on the sub-ject. Tonight with Mrs. Pilsudski worrying about getting home, she will wet our couch for sure, and, once she leaves, Ma will dab the cushion and say, "Be patient with her. Yes, she leaves open the bathroom door and pees a little on our couch, but she's old and can't help it."

"I'm going upstairs," I say.

"You should give us all a break," says Ma. "Go study your wildflowers."

With the Lake Superior wind blowing hard outside, I sort through dried weeds, tape them to cardboard squares, write beneath each its name—"Wild Rye," "Caraway," "Tansy." The weed-cards are fun. They pass the time for me like clipping newspaper items does. A brittle weed I collected once and mounted on cardboard, "Fireweed," also has a news clipping beside it that kind of matches it.

(From page 10, *Scrapbook*):

HOT UNDER THE COLLAR
Mourners smelled smoke at a funeral. When a mortician

investigated, he found a fire inside a coffin. Investigators said embalming fluid leaking from the body of 42-year-old John "Jack" Peters may have caused a chemical reaction, touching off the fire.

Another clipping reminding me of no one or nothing—and certainly of no weed—begins, "Ashland, Wisc. woman charged with adultery" (page 11, *Scrapbook*). It tells that "enforcement of an adultery law attracted worldwide attention and is raising questions about the old statute's constitutionality." Then you read how over-the-road truck driver B. M. Bertilson asked the district attorney to prosecute his wife "under the law that hadn't been used in Wisconsin in the 20th century." Mr. Bertilson said his wife, Lotty, admitted breaking the law while he was on the road far from Ashland. What weed or plant could complement this story—Pokeweed? Bouncing Bet? Aaron's Rod?

Another weed mounted on cardboard, Heal All, matches a news clipping that recalls Cousin Thaddeus. Page 13, *Scrapbook*, talks about a man dressed in robes and pulling a heavy wooden cross down the highway outside town. "SECOND COMING COULD BE IN NORTHLAND," reads the headline.

The article said a man yelled, "Praise the Lord," when a cop, who goes to our church, offered him assistance. Then, when the officer told him it was a highway hazard pulling this cross down the road, the newspaper article said the man offered "passive resistance," so Lieutenant Gunski arrested him and the cross. On the way to town, Lieutenant Gunski stored the cross in the East End gas station, back with the motor oils, then put the man in jail until his mother sent money to pay the fine. I made up a headline for this one: "CASE OF ARRESTED CROSS." But you don't read the real surprise until the end. When the man with the "dark blond hair pulled back in a ponytail" got out of jail and claimed his property, he placed the huge cross over his shoulder and trudged off. Only he'd rigged it so the walking was easier than it was on Jesus' long haul up Calvary. "He had a neat wheel on the back of it. Still, if you're dragging that sucker down the highway, it's got to be heavy," said the gas station owner, George Polkoski.

When snow is piled against the bedroom window and the cedar tree is bent far over from wet snow, more news comes, a banging on the front door—Souls of the Faithful Departed walking in the storm. Soon, cold air shoots upstairs.

"Hey, look-it this!" I hear Pa say.

He likes Thaddeus, who's just arrived but then suddenly disappears. Thaddeus is one of many servicemen, especially marines, to come from East End.

"Close the door you were breaking down out there a second ago," says Ma. "You are sure in a hurry to get inside, Tad."

As I head to the hallway at the bottom of the stairs, I watch Pani Pilsudski pulling an afghan over her shoulders. "Hey, where'd Tad go? He vanish from sight and become a dead soul?"

"I just told him to shut the porch door, that's all," Mother says.

"Good afternoon, everyone," Tad says. "You're darn right I wanted in. The thing I don't like about the dark is it's always dark. Geez, I took quite a fall outside."

Though Thaddeus is too young to drink, people buy him beer and wine. He's been on a rumba. A red-and-white wool tassel cap warms his ears. Over his haunted eyes rest blue, square-shaped sunglasses like the Byrds wear. He has on a knee-length, forest-green uniform overcoat with the red cloth patches on the sleeves showing he's a marine lance corporal. Snow sticks to one elbow and to the side of the coat. He's fallen down and looks crazy.

"I'm out of uniform. You're not suppose' to wear sunglasses. It ain't military," he says. "What stinks in here? You let one, Mrs. Pilsudski?"

"*Me*, I stink," says Pa. "It's the odorant so you know what a real gas leak smells like in your home appliances."

"We know what *you* smell like. Say," Tad asks, "what kind of kid collects weeds for a hobby? And newspaper clippings? This ain't normal." He waits a minute. "No, I don't think it *is* normal," he says, laughing.

My father stands in the archway between the kitchen and the living room. "How long you got left on your leave?" he asks.

"Tomorrow…tonight," says Tad. "All Saints' and Halloweenie."

"Then where you go be stationed?" asks Pani Pilsudski.

"I've told you one hundred times, Mrs. Pilsudski," Tad says. "Turn up your hearing aid."

"No, you haven't told us once," Ma says.

"Wounds affected your memory?" Pa asks. "Have you seen his Purple Heart, Mrs. Pilsudski? Our nephew here is suffering wounds."

She daydreams of something or someplace else and doesn't answer.

My mother sure doesn't think Tad's showing up here drunk is very funny. During her happily married life near the Northern Pacific ore dock, she's seen too many neighborhood men getting drunk, fighting, hollering, falling in the snow. It's like in the Old Country. A weekly Polish paper, the *Gwiazda Polarna*, recently reported how a cold wave killed thirty-six people in Poland. Most of them were drinkers who went outside or fell asleep in unheated rooms. Just two old women froze, I read.

When Tad takes the heavy marine overcoat off, we see how thin he's become.

"I'm going back to Vietnam," he says. "Can't eat nothing. Can't keep it down. Too worried."

When he removes his tassel cap, a line divides the tanned part of his face from the pale part. It's like this from his wearing a helmet three months ago. The pale part will never go away. I think he will be marked by this Vietnam War and a pale forehead forever.

"Got you a present, Edda," he says, pulling a bottle of vodka from the inside of the greatcoat. Next, he produces a paper he's kept beneath his jacket.

"Going back to Vietnam. Goddamn it, I'm going back."

"Well," Pa says, "you're sure gonna have the last laugh on us, because next week you'll be where it's hot and tropical."

"Over there it'll be the monsoon season when your clothes get moldy green fuzz on them. Your shoes rot, too. It's what I'm gonna call *you*, Andy—Fuzz Mold," Thaddeus says to me. "It's your new name."

"I like it," I say.

"Your weather'll be better than the siege of winter we're gonna get," says the gas man, my father. "It's starting early this year."

"I don't want to go. I made a mistake, Uncle Edda. I'm okay. I signed up for a tour. Goddamn. But I'm okay. I can't remember if I said I was going back or not. I forget everything these days. Here—"

The vodka he presents us looks slightly greenish in the bottle.

"Look, Andy!" says Pa.

In it is a stem of something. Thaddeus says, "European bison food. Distiller puts this herb in each bottle. It colors and flavors the product. 'Żubrówka' Bison Brand Vodka. I can't recall where I got it," he says. "Someplace where I was drinking last night. Read this to us, Andy Fuzz Mold."

The label says, "Flavored with an extract of the fragrant herb beloved by the European Bison," I read. I turn the bottle sideways. The herb floating in vodka hypnotizes us.

"Gimme," my pa says. "Let's look at it."

"You have to work, Edda. You can't drink," Ma says. Putting water glasses out for the vodka, she brings Mrs. Pilsudski her glass. "Jezu," I hear Pani exclaiming after one sip. After two, I hear her singing a radio commercial for this wine that's always advertised: "One sip of Arriba, and you, too, will hear the beat-beat-beat of the bongos."

With everyone drinking, everyone crazy, I think Tad looks great. He *is* cool. I don't call him a soldier; I call him a marine. A new kind of savage fighter in the Asian jungle, he dresses out of uniform and wears dark granny glasses, but despite what he looks like when he is home recovering from his wounds, he wants to win the war. I'm glad he is a member of the Boruczki clan, and I hope I can put him in my *Scrapbook of Brave Men* under the heading "Cousin Thaddeus Milszewski."

I ask him, "Do you want to go to Vietnam?"

"Oh no . . . oh sure," he says. "I've been wounded once. I'll fight like heck."

"Beat-beat go the bongos," says Pani. "Oo-la-la. Smell *goot* in house."

"It's all right if you're afraid to go back," Pa says. "I'm afraid some nights at the gasworks."

"I'm not afraid," Tad says.

"That's the spirit," says my dad, clinking glasses with Thaddeus. From the kitchen table, my crazy-looking cousin picks up the piece of paper he brought in. The folded map is a foot long, maybe ten or eleven inches wide. When he opens it into two halves, we see only the back part.

"Are you ready?" he asks. He drinks more vodka, nibbles a piece of herb. "You'll see a map of your life."

Pa sips his vodka. He gives me a drink of it in preparation for what Tad is going to show us.

Opening the paper to expose its four quarters, Thaddeus

keeps the blank side toward us. We see his eyes behind blue lenses, half-pale, half-tan face, his hands holding up the paper, which
he then turns.

"Wow!" I say. It has so many lines, dots, squares. There are
light blue and green places, pink and purple ones. You see thin
lines and circles drawn in black. The map unfolded is at least two
feet by two feet, I figure. When he spreads it out, the paper covers much of the kitchen table.

"What is it of?" I ask before I see that blue represents the
lakes and rivers of our home . . . of the "NE/4 Superior 15´
Quadrangle of Superior, Wisconsin."

"It's as topographic as I'll ever want to get," Tad says. "I
ordered it through the mail. I'm gonna educate the Viet Cong."

Overcoat off, he hangs his green uniform jacket on the back
of the kitchen chair, then smooths the jacket. His tie and shirt are
tan. The lance corporal rank insignias on the shirtsleeves are
darker green than the lime-green parts of the map. "The VC will
see and fear Superior, Wisconsin," my cousin says. "They will
learn to fear Superior, especially the East End. They will feel the
wrath of a true son of the East End."

"Take a drink," says Pa to me. "Say 'oo-la-la,' Andy. Smell
CH_4."

"I like the smell on your clothes, Pa," I say.

Nibbling herb, Tad says, "I need strength to go back there. It's
gonna take real guts to show them my wrath."

"You need a map of home," I tell Tad.

Among its various features are lime-green swamps and wet-
lands with blue tick marks to indicate marsh grass. You also see
our town in pink with symbols on it for churches like St. Adalbert's; symbols for schools, docks, railroad yards, sandpits, the
hospital, the cemeteries; for roads that cross through woods,
creeks, and swamps; for railroad trestles. One of the biggest trestles stands here by our house and Mrs. Pilsudski's. Finally on the

map are the creeks and blue rivers, one flowing to the southwest
and off the map, another flowing north past our house to the
bay, then out into the largest freshwater lake in the world.

Looking at the map, my cousin pours another drink. In the
living room, Ma and Mrs. Pilsudski talk about the weather.

"The leg?" Pa asks Thaddeus.

"Healed up okay. In two weeks, I'll be over there with this
map. Sprout," he says to me, "I'm going to promote you from a
nonentity to a private first class. 'To All Who Hear These Presents, Greetings,'" he says like he's reading a proclamation. Then
he gives me a blue booklet whose cover reads:

CONSTITUTION AND BY-LAWS OF THE THADDEUS
KOSCIUSZKO CLUB. COMPOSED OF ALL THE SLAVIC PEOPLE
IN THE SUPERIOR, WISC. AREA. ORGANIZED AUGUST IST,
1928

"I joined up," Tad says. "All you have to do is pay the membership fee, first year's dues of six dollars, and prove you're Polish,
which ain't hard in this neighborhood. I wanna lay claim to
being in the Polish Club of Superior. If I get killed in Vietnam,
then at least you'll always know I joined the club. I'll have a map,
too. It'll be close by so a medic can get it for me while I'm
dying. In the newspapers, you'll read about the casualty of a
hometown boy. Shit, I'm gonna have to leave home!" He kisses
the map. "Edda, the Purple Heart is authentic. They gave it to
me. But what did I get it for? I hate to tell you this. I might never
see you again. Geez, I've had too much beer tonight—I'm a
cook, Edda. Christ, like Mrs. Pilsudski or some Polish *baba*.
A cook! Never told no one. The guys like my cooking. They
ask for *pierogi* when they come back from search-and-destroy
operations near An Ho. *Pierogi*, of all things. Oh, I'm glad I joined
the club."

He is almost crying, but I know Tad is strong, and he is cool in sunglasses. Even Pa thinks so and will not accept that Tad is only a cook in the marines.

I take a sip of Tad's vodka.

"Andy, don't let them have no more in there," Ma calls to me. "And what are you doing with the men?"

"It's a map," I say. "Tad's got the Polish Club membership rules with him, too."

Trying to change the subject from Tad's culinary skills for the marines, my father points to the Nemadji River my cousin's just kissed. Pa is saying, "These lines show the height of hill and valley. You read the lay of the land by them. The purple waving lines, the contour lines, represent ten-foot intervals. Says so right here. You don't needa believe me, but you should believe what a map before you says on this very table in a Polish household."

Near where both my grandfathers rest in the cemetery, the Nemadji River, which translated from the Ojibwe means "Left-Handed River," sweeps in a wide blue arc on the topographical map. Flowing beneath the Chicago & North Western trestle, the river runs through a swamp, then past more neighbors' houses.

As Thaddeus bends to kiss another area of the map, I figure that, according to the contour lines, the land above the river must drop thirty feet as it nears the bay. All of this is marked on the map. Sometimes, in real life, the Left-Handed River reverses course. Instead of entering the bay from the south, the way it normally does, the river appears as if it's running back to where it came from. This happens when northwest winds create white-caps on the lake.

"If I kiss the place," Tad's saying, "then I'm okay. But how do you kiss a neighborhood? I've never done nothing brave. At least lemme study this map a little and get some strength."

"You'll be home soon. You'll be discharged," my father says.

Seeing the mark on the map where the water tower used to

be, I point to it, telling them to look. Pa must swallow his Żubrówka the wrong way, because he has to cough. "It's the old railroad water tower near the bay," he says. "'WT' means water tower. I forgot about it. Now my kid spots 'er. The round tank, the funnel that trains got water from. Great. You're some map reader, Andy," he congratulates me. "The water tower has been torn down for a long time."

"What's this on the map, the 'Pesthouse'?" I ask.

"It's not here anymore," he tells me.

"Am I here?" asks Tad. "Do I exist? Man, too much beer and vodka."

We study the map's contours as though they were contours of our lives, and Pa says, "In purple at the bottom it's got 'Revisions compiled and map edited 1964.' But over here . . . 'Topography from aerial photographs taken 1959.' It's 1968. I'm looking at 'er and seeing things have changed. No 'Home for the Aged.' No 'Poor Farm.' No 'Pesthouse.' Tore down so many years ago like other things. I suppose it's how they do things at a map company."

"I don't know why they sent me an old map."

Despite the map's insufficiencies, Tad kisses it again, and I wonder if I could ever feel such love for the East End.

It is strange when the church bell rings. At 6:00, storm or not, it rings everyday; but now the kitchen clock reads 6:07, and we're examining a map of old places, and the bell rings and startles me.

It must be the weather; snow changes contours. In winter blizzards, in summer heat, I've heard the bell as I explored beneath the trestle, floated in Burbul's canoe on the river, or walked over the ice on the bay before the first snow. I've heard the bell out on Hog Island and heard it at the cemetery above the Left-Handed River. Always at six o'clock. Now today, it rings late.

In the living room, Pani says, "Beat-beat." Her head falls. She dozes.

"Rivers don't change," Tad says. "Goddam. I've gotta do something brave. I want to be remembered as the East End man who wore a Purple Heart on his chest. Oh, this heart, Uncle Edda and Fuzz Mold! A crate of eggs fell on me. Then a barrel of S.O.S. on top . . . chipped beef, chunks of ground beef in a cream sauce. 'S.O.S.' is short for '*Sheet* on a shingle,' as Mrs. Pilsudski would say. There mighta been bread involved in this incident, five or six loaves. Sausage links. Oatmeal. They all fell. A food accident crushed me. I have the leg to prove it. We were going to the field to bring a meal to the grunts. We'd rewarm it when we got there. Intelligence said everything was hunky-dory on the road. They cleared us to go. Our convoy carried field stoves, food, ice for tea, immersion heaters for the troops to dip mess kits in hot water after chow—

"Staff Sergeant Farrazzi was up in the cab with the driver. We didn't rope stuff down good. Only the eggs were secured, but that didn't help. The driver swerved to miss a peasant walking his water buffalo. The peasant was heading through this storm swirl of butterflies, which the driver tried to avoid. The driver'd got his military license for that size of truck only a month before. Here I am a lance corporal who'd made many a tasty soufflé and who wanted his Belgian waffles to be the best in the Ninth Marine Expeditionary Brigade, and I'm wounded by eggs and bread. I'm drunk. Did you know Ho Chi Minh collected butterflies?"

"Don't talk none about war," my pop says. "You're my sister's boy. It is a shame you can't feel like a hero. I don't believe what you told us. You're no cook. You're a hero, even if you're drunk."

"I could make you something to eat," Thaddeus says. "Eggs and toast, kielbasa and eggs to prove my courage. Everybody likes Polish sausage."

"Won't kielbasa remind you of combat?" I ask.

"What are you talking about?" Mother asks as she comes into the room. "Get your cousin a cup of coffee right now, Andrew. He has to sober up. You all sound rattle-brained. Stop drinking before you get too crazy. Straighten up."

"He don't need coffee," says my father, pouring him a glass of Żubrówka as Tad tries to speak Polish. Outside, tree branches and pine boughs litter the snow. We sit in a kitchen where I think the contour of a life, the history of a life, must run like purple lines that show its depth, and I suddenly believe this map of Tad's should include other people who've lived in the East End of Superior and sat together on stormy nights in kitchens, as well as the people on the Old Country map you see at the Warsaw Tavern. Now Tad is making a place for himself on the map of memory. I am, too, thinking that among the storm's windfall of trees and branches this very All Saints' Eve, departed souls are waiting for another soul to depart—this one for Vietnam. Maybe it's storming in Old Country Poland now, too. It's possible, I think, that the herb connects us—the herb, our history, and this old Polish language Thaddeus is trying to speak.

Now Ma tells Pani Pilsudski, "Don't worry. We'll get you home."

Helping her up, Mother hugs her so she knows she's okay. As Mrs. Pilsudski puts on her wool coat and boots, I throw on a jacket, push open the porch door against the storm.

Between our house and hers, two feet of snow drift over the sidewalk. On the nearby railroad trestle, a train passes quietly. When we've crossed the new contours, Mrs. Pilsudski thanks us, tells us she will say a rosary for us. "Arriba," she says. "Beat-beat bongos."

"Arriba," we say. "Beat-beat."

I figure Thaddeus will now return to his map; but he goes off into the night wearing his tassel cap, blue sunglasses, and uniform overcoat—stumbling into the wind, maybe to his mother's home, maybe to the Polish Club. "I'm doing fine," he's saying.

I lose sight of him in the storm. As I walk back into the house, I see Pa stumbling a little but know he'll be okay.

I page through the blue booklet Tad gave me. Sixteen pages in Polish, a language I am trying to study but now need Pa's help to read. "*Celem Towarzystwa Bratniej Pomocy im. Tadeusza Kościuszki . . . ,*" it starts, then goes, "*będzie skupienie pod swój sztander Polaków, ku wzajemnemu I moralnemu poparciu. . . .*" "Look–it," I say, "'The Club's purpose is the gathering of Poles under their own standard for mutual and moral support.'" I read in Polish after Pa how the Kosciuszko Club and Lodge is also for "'the fostering among club members of the feeling of love and brotherhood, for the defending of Polish honor, and finally for the furtherance of the principles and immortal deeds of one of Poland's greatest sons.'"

"It's a symbol," Pa says.

"You're drunk, Edda," Mother says.

"Drinking'll kill me," says my father.

"Go to bed, Andrew," Ma says as the telephone rings.

I answer it. Mr. and Mrs. Novazinski are both talking at once: "Andy! Your cousin says he wants to kiss our walls and floors while he's out trick-or-treating. He never wants to leave East End, he says. We gave him some candy, told him to get going. Call his house. Tell his parents the kid's crazy drunk."

Handing Ma the phone, I go upstairs. I stare at my weeds. I read a little in my Polish heritage book. When people die in houses in the Old Country, it says, mirrors are turned in to face the wall, and windows are opened so the spirit isn't trapped inside the house.

Even though no one has died tonight that I know of, I still turn my mirror backward to the wall when the phone rings again.

It rings again later. It must be about Tad. Then my dad is in the next room getting ready for work.

"Hawkweed, Tansy, Goldenrod," I whisper to my collection. I quietly raise the window, then the storm window behind it to let out the spirits of the dead—or in Tad's case, the living. The warm air of spirits rushes out through the screen. I have followed the old custom.

Hearing Pa go downstairs, I stop whispering and think there is finally peace this night of souls, until a little while later I hear a pounding on the storm door. As I peer through the window into the swirling wind and snow, I see Thaddeus in uniform.

"It's me," he's saying, drunk, frightened. "It's Thaddeus. Remember where I stood on All Saints' Eve. Don't forget where I stood."

"You're no Kosciuszko, Tad," I say to him from my window.

"I know. I want to be. I want to win the war. I want to be a hero." He's holding open a paper bag. "See? This is a start. I got a bag full of candy. I can do great things if I set my mind to it."

Downstairs, the phone rings again. I hear Ma's voice through the furnace register. "Tad, people are calling about you," I yell out to him. "They say you're kissing their houses, you're kissing their porches and steps . . . even their doors and mailboxes. Your folks are pretty angry. My pop sure is, with the phone ringing so much. Be careful out there, will ya, Tad? Don't drink no more. Don't go trick or treating no more."

"I won't," he says.

He kneels down to clear the snow with his hands. I see the earth underneath that he loves. I see this one dark spot in the world of white. He is uncovering the center of the world.

When Pa steps outside on his way to the gas plant, crazy Tad, like he can't take his hands from the cold earth of northern Wisconsin, is working at the snow, saying, "I knelt here once.

Remember me. Remember where I stood and knelt. Remember the earth I kissed just as winter came."

When Pa looks down, Tad says, "I'll show the Viet Cong something they'll never forget. Oo-la-la, war is hard."

Still stumbling from the Żubrówka, now Pa kicks at the snow to clear a little more away, as if this could keep Thaddeus in the East End forever.

Time Between Trains

FIVE DAYS A WEEK, the track inspector checked the rail line from the Superior waterfront up to Chub Lake. During summer and autumn dry spells, he worked weekends looking for fires set by sparks from train wheels. From the cab of his rail truck, he spotted undercuts, washouts, and fires in the tinder-dry grass, reporting them to the radio dispatcher at the railyard in Superior. Joe Rubin extinguished small fires himself. With a track warrant for every portion of his trip, he went along in the special truck that had rubber tires for road and highway travel and flanged, locomotive-style wheels for railroad travel. To switch from one to the other mode, he would center the truck at a railroad crossing, climb down, grab a metal pole to insert into the wheel mechanism, and raise the steel, flanged wheels, leaving the rubber tires resting on the track. Backing up the truck, he would stop, turn the steering wheel, drive forward, and be back on dirt or pavement.

In his fourteen years with the Burlington Northern–Santa Fe, Joe Rubin looked for sun kinks, broken rails, broken bonds, wooden ties left on the tracks, and other potentially deadly defects or impediments on or alongside the way to Chub Lake.

When Joe Rubin reported a sun kink (when the sun expands a steel rail, bending it out of place), the section crew got after it. When he reported a pull apart (in bitter cold, railroad tracks contract and can pull apart), the section crew came to lay kerosene-soaked ropes next to the rails and waited for the heated track sections to snap together.

Along the east-west tracks before the Crawford Creek signals (where flashing yellow means a track inspector can move onto the main line at Saunders) were the broken ties he reported one day last November. West of there was a section of track ballast to keep an eye on near that boggy run before the Vet's Crossing. Farther along, past Boylston, almost to the signal lights at Milepost 15.9 where the tracks converge, was the hair-thin rail fracture in the right rail of eastbound track he reported last December. How important this work! Thank God for the track inspector.

Naturally, his job required keen senses. In a noisy diesel locomotive pulling twenty-two thousand tons of taconite from the Hibbing, Minnesota, plant down past Kelly Lake terminal to the Superior dock, sometimes a railroad engineer can also sense discrepancies in a track. But Joe Rubin was supposed to be first to identify when a track sounded off. He was regional Employee of the Month twice during his fourteen years. The award meant much to him, for unlike many employees, he lived for the railroad. Mornings, he cleaned his BN hardhat of grease or dirt, whispering absent-mindedly to himself about a section of track he had to examine. Friday evenings, in the kitchen of his apartment by the railyard, he reviewed his week's performance. The work week over, he was likely to talk aloud to his parents' pictures on the walls of his rooms. On the second and fourth Wednesdays of the month, he got a haircut. All of these were solitary activities, for he wasn't one to say much to a barber.

His week, his life, was made solitary in other ways. He'd had very few girlfriends over the years, which meant no one to telephone about meeting for a drink or going to dinner. He was probably the only Jewish track inspector in a vast BN-SF railroad network stretching from here to Fort Worth, and he drove the truck eight hours a day through such long stretches of uninhabited country that he might as well have been in Siberia. BN section hands called him the Wandering Jew. Wanderer or not, this was lonely work. The tracks ran through miles of speckled alder rising black against the snow—through aspen and pine forests, past tamarack bogs and cutover hayfields, out over trestles where you saw frozen rivers meander below. Here and there appeared farmhouses and railroad crossings, but once he had his track warrant on a winter morning and was passing under Tower Avenue westbound on Number 1 main track, he pretty much said good-bye to everyone but the dispatcher. When he was stopped at a crossing or off on a siding while a 170-car taconite train came highballing down Saunders' Grade on the mainline, he'd wave to the engineer; but there was no talking, no laughing with a fellow employee, just Joe Rubin in freshly pressed work clothes standing on the shaking earth or sitting alone in his truck as the brown rail cars thundered past, trailing steam from taconite so hot from the mill that, even parked in the yards, unloaded boxcars steamed for three days.

With the last cars flown by, blinking safety light gone out of sight around a curve, quiet returned to the track inspector. Chickadees sang in the aspen trees. Crows circled above. A flock of snow buntings in a quiet cloud rose out of the stark gray branches of a mountain ash. After the train's passing, which probably disturbed Joe Rubin less than it did the wildlife, he called the dispatcher. "What you got going west? Number ninety-two BN-SF is by me now. Can I get a warrant to Chub Lake?" To which the dispatcher might reply, "I've got a tac train coming out of Allouez dock. I'll be holding a coal train at Chub Lake. You got an hour. Get coffee if you have a place nearby." More often than one might imagine, track inspectors have time between trains.

Though from certain mileposts, Joe Rubin could have raised the flanged wheels and made it to a country café and back, he generally brought a thermos of coffee and a sack lunch to eat. With his windows rolled down, what things he saw on mild winter days as he waited dreamily for the through freight: a spider made its way over the snow by his front tire; an ermine popped its head from the white earth; a snowy owl perched atop a paper birch, looking at the curious world. The delicate, beautiful bird and animal tracks he saw after a fresh snow reminded him of his own work on the tracks. When Joe Rubin drove his truck into the silent void after a train passed, it was as if it had never been there—no shrill whistle frightening deer, no diesel smoke—just the smooth gliding of the track inspector on his way to Chub Lake.

•   •   •

Early one year, he decided he'd become *too* committed to the railroad. Through his heavy boots, his legs, even up into his heart, he sensed the slightest problems with tracks. Nothing was too fine to escape the inspector's attention. He took good care of the truck; he worked late; he reported problems before they occurred. He wanted so much to be Employee of the Month again, that week after long week he thought of nothing else.

After work on Fridays he would stop in a place where he could be less vigilant of the railroad for an hour. Seeing Joe Rubin, someone would yell to Ogy, the bartender, as he rang up a cash register sale, "Play that Jewish piano, Ogy. Make the Jewish piano sing." The track inspector laughed as was expected of him, for he wanted to get along. But what some wiseguy yelled to the bartender coupled with "the Wandering Jew" nickname and other small slights made him feel that he might just as well go back out to inspect the tracks again. Listening to the sound of rails wasn't so bad, he told himself. He might as well spend the weekend in his truck on a siding, maybe at Milepost 8 or M.P. 12.

• • •

At M.P. 15.9 lived a woman who wished she were less solitary. Alone most evenings, this Sofia had done well in life, at least for Superior. She was a teacher in an elementary school outside town, eight miles east of her home. "Mrs. Stepan," the children called her, though she was a widow, and her married name now had a hollow ring to her ears.

She lived at the four corners where South Irondale Road crosses County Trunk Highway C, then winds through thick woods down into a river valley.

Sofia's house was the only building at the corners. Across the highway and the BN-SF tracks was the wooden M.P. 15.9 sign and the gray railroad masts that told east- and westbound trains to hold or proceed. In midsummer when everything greens up, the area is unremarkable, unnoticeable. In other corners of the intersection were ditches dug out of the clay, a few scraggly alder and hawthorn bushes, and miles of fields that ended in the woods where, forty years ago, her father hunted rabbits. Twenty times a day trains passed—every five minutes a truck or automobile on the paved highway came close to the house, but nothing slowed, nothing stopped except once in awhile a train on Number 1 track being held until the eastbound line was clear. Otherwise nothing, no reason to stop, though sometimes a truck driver speeding by might wave if he spotted Sofia staring out her bedroom window on the highway side of the house. At least there was something to see that way. Her other windows looked out on empty fields.

Five days a week during the school year she was at school—and then there was summer school in June and July. Sofia loved her third-graders; but after teaching them and reading to them, correcting arithmetic and penmanship, escorting them to the playground, coordinating milk breaks, meeting parents, taking care of the small and large responsibilities of a teacher's day, she found the job growing more tedious every year. For twenty-five years she'd done the work. During the January that Joe Rubin fully realized the extent of his commitment to *his* job, concentrating on railroad tracks to the exclusion of everything else, Sofia stared from her bedroom window and wondered where the years had flown. Her husband, Jerry Stepan, had been dead ten years, she had two women-teacher friends she saw socially once a month, and she lived alone in her house with shiplap siding at a boring crossroads in a flat country above a river valley. With a class of eight-year-olds clamoring for her attention, Sofia had less time than the track inspector for introspection. Still, as much of her time as they took and as much as she delighted in the children, she knew her life was passing.

As she daydreamed out at the fields, sometimes her life seemed so empty, but then she would snap herself out of her reverie and return to her pupils' work or listen to records as she reheated coffee in a pan on the stove. Maybe everyone feels this way in winter, she thought. Sofia had a few moments in the evenings to think like this, or on weekends after finishing the dishes and preparing her school clothes, but the track inspector, during every long season, had plenty of time to worry over where his life was going.

Though neither knew it, they traveled parallel tracks. The highway runs beside the tracks (except for the ditch between) until "Shortcut Road," where Sofia turned down a dirt road to pick up South State Highway 35 to school. Four or five times a year as he was heading to Chub Lake and she was on the way to or from Nemadji Elementary, they rode close to each other, the proximity occurring more often when he had time between trains—for the tracks at M.P. 15.9 are only a few steps farther from the house than from the highway. To Joe Rubin what did it matter that sometimes there was a woman driving parallel to him at the same speed he was going? Since the old neighborhood of Jews on Connors' Point had vanished, he thought there was no one worth noticing. His people had intermarried or moved away—everyone but the track inspector, who'd put off marriage to care for his parents. When his father died, the synagogue closed; the remaining old people went to Adas Israel in Duluth. Right before his mother died, the boarded-up Hebrew Brotherhood Synagogue in Superior (where his parents once had to reserve seats during High Holidays because of the large turnout of people) was set on fire. Over and over in the last weeks of her life, his mother said to Joe, "This isn't how it should end." As if to support her claim, her burial left the Hebrew Cemetery filled to capacity.

Busy as he was, Joe Rubin didn't often go to visit his parents' graves, and there was nothing left to see of the synagogue.

• • •

He concerned himself with a different kind of particulars now. He'd become a detective of sorts. At work he carried with him a small book. In some dreary northern place, when he got out of the truck to stretch, he compared pictures of animal tracks in the book to tracks he saw in ditches and fields, or sometimes running along or between the railroad tracks. Sometimes these mammal tracks made exquisite designs. Magnified, the smallest of them—shrew tracks—looked like hands with long, crooked fingers growing sharp and thin at the end. He learned that "long-tailed shrews frequently leave a tail mark on their trail, which is barely over one-inch wide." During the course of his investigation, he read in *Mammals of the Superior National Forest* that "red fox prints appear as a line of prints as if the animal were walking along a string. A fox track is roughly circular and 1.5–2 inches in diameter. In soft snow where detail cannot be seen, their tracks appear as a line of round depressions."

Sometimes he confused mammal tracks with the tracks made by birds' claws. The way they went out over the fields, on out into the distance, all these (if you pretended) could be the tracks of people like the wandering inspector. The variety of mice living in the area presented problems in track identification, too. Above the snow and tunneling beneath it, they left an artistic network Joe Rubin got on his knees to observe. What was so unusual about his kneeling in snow? Joe wondered. Old-time railroad workers broke out a pint of brandy or a couple of miniatures of whiskey or vodka to keep *them* company. At least what Joe Rubin did endangered no one. Kneeling in his brown jacket and insulated pants, he looked as if he were praying as he searched for the animal tracks, which, to him, seemed to represent the Diaspora of the Jews.

As he was doing this searching that resembled praying one afternoon when the schools celebrated Martin Luther King Jr.'s birthday and when he himself waited for a taconite train to pass, a voice startled him. The trackbed, the tracks, the gray signal masts looked especially forlorn. All morning a biting wind ducked low over the fields. Now this voice— "You grow to be like the company you keep."

Turning, he saw a woman in the middle of Number 2 track.

She said it again in what he thought must be Polish, "You become like the company you keep ... *Z kim przestajesz takim się stajesz.*"

She walked down the slight pitch in the road, crossed the highway, and went into her house, wondering, the teacher, why she hadn't walked toward the river on her day off. She sat a half-hour in her coat and gloves pondering it.

Now that he had seen her, she wouldn't catch him so deep in thought again.

When he heard her call to the rural mail carrier one afternoon, "Yes, it's a nice day," several months had passed. He'd traveled hundreds of miles round-trip from Superior to Chub Lake. He'd seen the spring sun erase mouse and hare tracks in the snow. He'd even noticed willows along the route turning yellow. Their leaves would appear in a month.

Two nights in February, on the other hand, she'd stayed at school for open house. One night in March, she had drunk too much Irish coffee, finding herself staring at the M.P. 15.9 sign. Another night that month, she had reread all her husband's letters, whispering "Jerzy" in Polish.

In April, when the wind is sharp (wind that sounds like her husband's name), then in the shelter of ditches bloom delicate cowslips, which her husband had called marsh marigolds. He'd ask in letters from Buffalo, New York, or Lorain, Ohio, "Are the marsh marigolds blooming, Sofia?"

"The cowslips, don't you mean?" she'd answer, jokingly.

He never bothered to correct her. A wheelsman on the ore boat *William F. Sutter*, he drowned in a Lake Michigan storm when the marsh marigolds were blooming back home. As a widow she learned that the chaliced, yellow flowers with heart-shaped leaves really are called marsh marigolds as often as cowslips. Each year for the ten years since her husband's death, they bloomed. Each April she was sad.

She didn't know the track inspector's name, but on her way to school, she was aware of his truck on the tracks paralleling the highway. She knew from a lifetime of learning important and unimportant facts that James J. Hill, the Empire Builder, had brought the railroad through here in the late 1800s, that her dear mother came from a part of Poland now called Silesia, that Douglas County has high unemployment, that a *bulbul* is a Persian bird, that the moisture content of hay in silos has to be checked to be sure that the hay doesn't combust, that cowslips are marsh marigolds, and that during the Middle Ages, Poland was a haven for Jews. She knew this last like she knew what a trapezoid is—or a parallelogram (her husband had accumulated compasses, rulers, protractors). What she knew about Catholic Poland and the Jews, that miscellaneous fact, would matter to Joe Rubin and the teacher. Now in a gusty April, however, she sat in the place where roads cross, the lonely four corners where, with nothing stopping it, the wind sweeps along without regard for anything.

When she was thinking of the track inspector—which she did at odd moments, happy to know that if he was at M.P. 15.9 then her house would be safe from intruders—the wanderer was thinking of her. When he had time, he'd surprise her, stand at the crossroads, wave to her. What did she mean saying he would become like the company he kept when he had no company? He imagined he saw those who really mattered, the people of the Diaspora, in the winter prints and tracks, in the forest shadows when the snow left, in the brown grass of fields, in the pictures on his walls. He could trace them back to Noah. His ancestors had remained four hundred and thirty years in Egypt. Such was the company Joe Rubin kept! If he hadn't found a home and still wandered the earth, enduring hardship and insult, such was his lot, he told himself as he radioed the dispatcher for a track warrant.

• • •

The one thing Sofia Stepan did with delight was to grow a garden out of sight of the railroad tracks and the county trunk highway. Except for this garden, she in no other way indulged herself. Though the garden stood in sunlight all afternoon on the south side of the house, by six o'clock—no matter the warmth of the day—it was cool and quiet. There she grew aster, yarrow, phlox, black-eyed Susan, hollyhock, butterfly bush. Coreopsis and lantana were not unknown to her. From flower to flower fluttered cabbage butterflies, mourning cloaks, monarchs, swallowtails. One afternoon she counted sixty-five butterflies. Sofia thought the butterflies could impart something of their beautiful delicacy to you in proportion to how much peace and strength you needed after a decade of disappointments.

Though Joe Rubin hadn't seen her garden, he thought of the woman at the crossroads often. In May, convinced that the language she spoke was Polish and that she appeared to like seeing him at the crossroads, he thought of no one but her. One evening in the Hebrew Cemetery, where he hadn't been in months, he wondered exactly what kind of company *she* kept, this Polish woman. The names on the gravestones echoed his question—Lurye, Sher, Vogel, Pomush, Edelstein, Kaner, Cohen, Marcovich, Handlovsky. . . . The old people knew Polish. They'd lived in Poland. "You become like the company you keep."

As is customary, atop his parents' graves he placed a few stones from the cemetery road. They symbolized a rock-strewn desert landscape and how all are equal in death. He gathered a few stones to keep in his pocket. He prayed for his parents' souls, spoke aloud to them as the warm, spring breeze swept through the willow groves along the river below the cemetery. Stones on a grave are more permanent than flowers.

On the way home, he decided the next time the Polish woman was at work he would cross the highway and walk down Irondale Road past her house. What was the harm in going by her place? Jews and Poles had lived together for centuries.

Before he had a chance to do so, it was June. Her garden had been transformed by gentle rains, by the warm sun on the side of the house no one saw. As the third week of summer school passed, there were more butterflies in Sofia's garden than she'd ever seen. The flowers and bushes she planted attracted them. She wanted to read her husband's letters to them all day long; but in addition to a morning filled with teaching, she'd agreed to perform certain administrative tasks in the afternoon. When she finished, she hurried home.

She was still at school when Joe Rubin saw the company she kept. Even from the road, he couldn't believe his eyes. Flying about, carried on slight, warm breezes, the butterflies in Sofia's garden looked like rich silk. They tumbled and fluttered, purple, yellow, orange, blue, lighting on the flowers, glancing against the bright, delighted leaves. No one but Joe Rubin saw them, in his pocket the stones from the cemetery, which in his amazement he left on the road in front of her house and in her yard.

When she returned home at four o'clock, she thought at first it was Jerzy in the butterfly garden. "Jerzy?" she cried, thinking her theory was right about the peace and strength butterflies bring to those in need. She thought her husband had brought her a letter.

When she saw who it really was, however, and that this was no sailor's ghost of Jerzy Stepan with a love letter, her heart fell for just a moment, but then she murmured, "That's all right. You can come in," to the trespasser, to the man who looked for mouse, hare, and fox tracks in winter and who now gently swept the butterflies from his shirt and hands.

Holy Walker

PANI PILSUDSKI kept a busy professional and social calendar. Today she had a nun's aching feet to soothe, then a rosary sodality meeting to lead in prayer. She hurried over the railroad trestle and around the edge of Novack's barley field. "Call me Pilsudski, the Wetter, do they, Pilsudski, the Couch Dampener!" She imagined the ladies whispering other slanderous things about her. Ceil Zawacki would say, "She permanently crippled and disabled Alec Mihalek when she repaired his callus. Do you see how he limps? Guess what else, girls? When she got up from our love seat, she left a wet spot I had to clean with spot remover." Mrs. Pilsudski, who battled fluid retention and whose poor, swollen legs bothered her, knew Barbara Trianowski would start in next: "That's nothing. She never flushes our toilet."

Lies! Lies! Terrible lies! thought the old widow who struggled to do God's work on her knees with such tools as a paring knife and a basin of water.

She'd come to *your* house if your feet bothered you. Despite her good intentions about your feet, it was very easy for her to make mistakes. She lived alone in a big, gray house hard by the railroad trestle. Over the years its front porch had heaved from frost, so that you climbed up three steps, then descended four or five inches to the door. If you left the front door open one minute, inside doors squeaked and swung shut the next, because, over decades, the winter cold had shifted the ancient foundation. Then, too, the upstairs rooms shook so from passing freight trains that Mrs. Pilsudski had to grab the headboard of her bed to steady herself. The house seemed confused, bewildered. Was it a railroad depot or was it Mrs. Pilsudski's house? When C&NW freights rumbled past, it was like heaven was falling into tumult. Crucifixes on the wall shuddered; statues of Mary and Joseph toppled. The shrine of St. Anthony of Padua once marched two feet across the top of her cedar chest to jitterbug with St. Jude, Patron of Lost Causes.

The freight trains contributed to her shaking hands; maybe they were the reason she retained water, because she was so nervous all the time—then a slip of the knife, then a cry of pain, then a customer's toe to bandage. If her mistakes continued, she'd lose people's trust. When it all got too much, the widow stared at herself in a mirror and wept. "*Starość nieradość,*" she'd exclaim. "Old age is no good." The loneliness, too. If she didn't keep the television on to distract her, she'd think all day how life conspired against her.

Lord, how much there was to dwell on. She still hated the sodality women for bringing up an old story about her. During Mass once, she'd had to make a quick exit. In the ladies' room, she pulled down her living girdle to relieve herself of what she called "water buildup." As she hurried back to receive communion, a lengthy piece of toilet paper clung to her skirt. Though Mrs. Pilsudski concentrated on the Body of Our Savior during this sacred moment, on the trip back to her pew, people snickered, altar boys laughed. The parish was still laughing, because certain sodality women couldn't shut up about the toilet paper that'd looked like a miniature bridal train. Even the priest at coffee hour said to her as though she were Mr. Whipple, "Don't squeeze the Charmin, Stella."

"Jezu *kochanej,*" she muttered, embarrassed even now at the memory.

At home she'd rouged her cheeks, pulled her gray hair into a bun, put on eyeglasses that pinched her ears. Despite resistance from her girdle, she'd pushed her body forward to work her feet into good, solid shoes. Finally, out came the wool coat she wore year round. Thus prepared, she set out across the trestle above the Left-Handed River, gradually coming to her wits' end what with the heat and with the heavy work and social pace she'd been setting for herself.

Clear of the trestle now and of the barley field where in the fall she picked caraway seeds to chew on the way to Mass, she spied St. Adalbert's Church and across from it the school with its gymnasium where the sodality circle met. She felt the coat hang heavily from her shoulders. Something else hung in her mind: the demons who would talk about her and her wet spot, Baba this, Baba that. The main thing was that *she*—the once envied, respected Mrs. Pilsudski—was leading rosary sodality tonight, and there was nothing they could do about it.

Each so-called Rose, or worship group, was here. She heard the good Polish ladies of Rose One chattering in the school gym downstairs; the Lithuanians of Rose Two; the Slovaks of Rose Three. (Oh, those Slovaks irritated her using their word *sokol* instead of the proper English word *sodality*. Harriet Bendis especially got to her the way she always played up to the priest.) On and on Mrs. Pilsudski counted how many Slovaks were here, how many Lithuanians, how many Poles.

Upstairs above the classroom and gym, Sister Dorota in coif and wimple sat on a couch with white lace doilies. Wiping the remains of a heavy supper from her chin, she wiggled her toes in the warm water of the metal pan Mrs. Pilsudski kept with the nuns.

"How are your feet?" inquired the podiatrist when she came in, out of breath from climbing the stairs.

Falling heavily to her knees, she swished water in the basin, trying to concentrate on the rosary sodality. But all she could think of was the thief and grocer Harriet, the Slovak the ladies called Jadzia, who'd recently presented the old church a new confessional. *Jadzia, Jadzia*, she hated the name! "If Jadzia's behind the counter at her store and you order a pound of wieners and are just a little over, Sister, she'll break one with her thumb and throw the piece back in her meat cooler. What *goot's* a half-inch long wiener to Jadzia? 'Mrs. Bendis,' I always say to her, 'I pay for wienie. Don't break it t'at way.'"

"Ow," Sister said when Mrs. Pilsudski nicked her toe as though it were a wiener on Mrs. Bendis's grocery scale.

"Here. It's not bleeding. We'll soak it," said the bunion scraper.

She cut around on the nun's other foot, feeling privileged to do such humble service—like Mary Magdalene would. She cut off a slice of callus like a slice of pear. She scraped at Sister's other calluses.

"I have sodality meeting," Mrs. Pilsudski said a moment later as she washed her hands in the kitchen. "I'm tonight's leader."

Hoping for the nun's blessing, she heard only the four other nuns discussing their favorite TV reruns. Mrs. Pilsudski powdered her face. A light blue ribbon hung from the sodality pin above her heart. She adjusted the ribbon and pin.

Taking a breath, she corrected her posture. Though she didn't fear leading the women in the Apostles' Creed, she did fear the Hail Mary. *That* prayer would confuse her, for lately—no, it'd been a year or two already—she'd been saying the rosary without thinking what the prayers meant. At home she'd pray with the TV on reruns of *Mister Ed* or *Green Acres*. Her lips would move reverently, fingers edging along the beads, but her mind would be lingering on what Mister Ed said to Wilbur. In the middle of the Hail Mary, she'd laugh at how they made the horse's lips move or she'd sing the *Green Acres* theme.

At sodality she'd lose her concentration, too. It never failed. While other ladies bowed, she'd stare at Mrs. Waletzko's dishpan hands or calculate how much hair Mrs. Simrak had lost.

"It's 'Hail Mary, full of *the* grace, the Lord is with Thee, blessed art Thou amongst *the* women, and blessed is the Fruit of Thy Womb, Jesus,' not 'Hail Mary, Mother of God, pray for us sinners . . . ,'" she told herself. She always got the Hail Mary and the Holy Mary mixed up. That was what came of watching TV nonstop: you didn't pay attention to your rosary. Fifteen times she said it: "Hail Mary, full of the grace—"

Downstairs, forty-five sodality women waited. Each, according to the rules, was to say three rosaries by herself per week, one for each of the three mysteries of the rosary.

Each mystery contained five smaller ones, such as the Mystery of the Presentation of Jesus in the Temple.

Checking behind her to see that no baby-soft Charmin stuck to her, Mrs. Pilsudski peeked in. The newest sodality members sat at the lower end of the warped hardwood floor, the older ones at the gym's other end. Someone was saying, "Baba," thought Mrs. Pilsudski, but overcoming her fear, she marched in. "Prayer time," she said. After hurried talk and the rustling of glass, plastic, and wooden beads, each Rose held the crucifix of her rosary.

The Apostles' Creed and the Our Father passed smoothly. As Mrs. Pilsudski began the first of ten small beads with "Hail Mary," though, a spiteful voice cut her off.

Forty-four selfless voices responding to the Hail Mary, and one selfish voice had to rush her response.

Mrs. Pilsudski tried again. "Hail Mar—." Before she finished, the voice said, "Holy Mary, Mother of God," in perfect English. Two beads deep and it was a prayer war.

The widow had heard that annoying, urgent voice for years at the grocery store saying, "It'll be forty-five cents for this" or "sixty-three cents for that." Now Mrs. Pilsudski was hurrying to get away from it. The faster she, Stella Pilsudski, said, "Hail Mary," the faster the other woman's voice: "Holy Mary."

"Hail Mary." "Holy Mary." "Hail Mary." "Holy Mary." It was a holy race.

Jadzia, the conserver of wieners, exalted herself with each response, which was just like her. She was wearing a summer suit, sensible for tonight's weather, conceded Mrs. Pilsudski, though perhaps a bit formal. The corner grocery store magnate had had her hair fixed, too. The bouffant did little for that turned-up snout. Now the widow Pilsudski's own hair fell about her forehead in sweaty ringlets. Her winter dress trapped the summer heat. She could feel her hands and legs swelling with water, her head growing light.

"Hail Mary, pray for us, the sinners," she said. "No, Hail Mary, I mean, full of the grace. That's what I mean."

"Holy Mary," the ladies were saying when the widow couldn't remember offering up a "Hail Mary." She and her living girdle weren't breathing right.

Knowing how the Lord suffered in the garden, she resolved to suffer herself and struggled through ten beads, through an Our Father, then through two more beads.

When the air got thick in the gym, she was moaning, "Hail Mary, Who art in heaven, Green Acres is the place for me."

"Stella-dear. Stella," they were saying, coaxing her back to consciousness. Someone opened the gym windows.

"Thy kingdom come, Thy will be done," the widow kept on, then muttered how much she liked Eva Gabor, even though Eva was Hungarian. She felt drowsy . . . couldn't for the life of her recall the character Pat Buttram played on *Green Acres*. The ladies lifted and fanned Mrs. Pilsudski's hair after they undid the bun. Even Harriet dabbed a wet handkerchief to the widow's flushed temples.

"I'm okay. Get away wit' that hankie. I saw a horse. I experienced a miracle. God on a horse. The horse neighed. A Polish horse, not Slovak!"

"You forgot your prayer, Stella. You were saying the Apostles' Creed, then talking about *Green Acres*. You dear thing, doing God's bidding like this."

"No, a talking horse," Mrs. Pilsudski said. "The owner's Wilbur. T'at's it, it's Wilbur."

The ladies congratulated her on her suffering and devotion to prayer.

"I always do what I can," said Mrs. Pilsudski humbly.

She wished the praise would continue until she realized how foolish she must look slumped over, head lolling, glasses steamed up. She was angry that Jadzia Bendis, a poker and pincher of frankfurters, had gotten to her.

When Mrs. Pilsudski stood up, she felt something. Oh, Lord! She couldn't look down at the "wetting accident." All the time smiling nervously, she grabbed her coat, side-stepped to the wall.

"Stella, stay for coffee," said Harriet.

"No coffee, no coffee," said Stella, then mouthed the word *ac-ci-dent*.

She wrapped the coat about her. God help me, I *am* a *baba*! she thought as she made her way out, for strength touching the sodality ribbon and pin that honored the Blessed Virgin.

Though completely done in, she managed to make her way down Third Street through the field onto the trestle. With no train coming, it was a clean walk home. A wooden railing rose from the walkway beside the trestle tracks. On one side was the forest and the river's long curve through it. Often from her kitchen window she'd watched people come across the trestle, just as someone could be watching her this very moment, huffing and puffing, the setting sun at her back. Maybe Mr. Boruczki, the neighbor, was drinking vodka and watching her before he went to his night shift at the gas plant. Or maybe Joseph Lesczyk was watching from the hill.

So this was God's punishment of the faithful: wetting your favorite girdle, she thought. When I've given so much to the poor and offered Christian witness through podiatry work, why this? When she tried recalling exactly what charitable work she'd done, though, she shamefully recalled pulling down the shades when she spotted the March of Dimes lady making her neighborhood collection. When Stella'd heard the lady knocking at the door, she hadn't answered. Later she spent the money she should have given to charity on a facial scrub and a loofah brush at Walgreen's. She did the same when "Jerry's Kids" knocked for Muscular Dystrophy. Who was *really* close with her money, though? Harriet Bendis was!—the Jadzia that God "punished" by giving her a corner grocery store, while she, poor Stella, scraped people's feet for a living.

The widow recalled a million terrible things about Harriet, such as the time, one summer evening, that Mrs. Respectability gave her, Stella, a head of cabbage from her garden for free, a present, but then at the end of the month she found on her grocery bill: "Head of Cabbage, Price—Fifty Cents." Calluses, nuns, bouffants, sodalities; she was through with them all. And she was really through with Jadzia!

Angry at having been embarrassed, she took the sodality pin from her dress, looked over the side, then dropped it from the trestle. The blue ribbon floated down, landing in muddy water. Mrs. Pilsudski watched it spin out of sight before she headed home thinking how—though it might offend the Church—she would extend her podiatry practice to Baptists and Lutherans.

For years she'd come this way to Bendis's market, to footcare patients' homes, to church, to sodality. She'd taken care of her feet; others neglected theirs. Now the lot of them could suffer the sorrow and heartbreak of burning, itching feet, she was thinking spitefully when she heard the whistle.

Until it blew again, she couldn't tell the direction. At the end of the trestle, the tracks curved through the trees. You couldn't see far ahead. Behind her now, though, a beam of light bounced up and down.

Heavenly Mary, more than half a trestle to go, she thought, and the whistle blowing for the crossing on the avenue. She tried walking faster, but it was so hard. Her glasses steamed up. Oh, Lord, that whistle! She concentrated on a rusted bolt holding the wooden guard railing together. Clutching the railing, she felt herself grow wetter. A minute later, the living girdle was newly soaked. Onto the trestle rattled the engine—hopper car, tank car, flatcar. From the terrifying whistle alone, the trestle would shake apart, she thought. Her hands clutching the railing, she remembered her missal lesson: "When hands are occupied, indulgences for saying the rosary may be gained as long as the beads are on one's person." Fearful of losing a grip on the railing, she couldn't get to her rosary.

"Ouch!" she cried, feeling sharp pain as the locomotive rumbled past. Her poor heart seemed to burst. Petrified, she looked at the sky through the diesel smoke, felt the rusted bolt moving as though it would come out and the entire trestle fall into the river and float down to the abandoned ore dock.

"Ow," she kept saying. "Ouch. Oh, God. Ow," she said. Each

time a boxcar passed, she remembered a sin she'd hidden from others and from the priest.

The train came, cars swaying, clicking. "Make me a rose in Your service," she said to God as an empty flatcar threw sawdust in her face, then a tank car with a yellow crust of sulfur and the words HYDROGEN SULFIDE rolled toward her. Now a tank car with CLAY SLURRY written on it. Now one with bauxite that blew more dust into her face. Now another car with INHALATION HAZARD painted on it. "Ow! Ouch!"

She stood dumb a moment. Another click. The rails stilled. Prying loose her fingers, she inched a step forward to see whether her legs could hold her up. Beyond the widow's house, the train blew for the crossing. Now it was quiet, as if a haze, a blue veil, had descended over the earth and over the widow.

Mist formed above the Left-Handed River. The moon rose. The air looked so blue and fresh, she thought. For the first time, she felt at peace.

A mystery, a blessed mystery of Christ!—kneeling before the nun, leading prayer, being struck dumb with anger and pride, the ordeal with the locomotive. Throughout all of this, she believed she'd grown even more beautiful, a faithful, dewy rose of Christ whose sins had been forgiven.

It was a splendid evening, cool enough now that the coat felt good. Frogs sang. Lightning bugs flitted among the trees. Lake boats far off in the harbor blew their whistles; the tugs responded. Familiar, comforting sights and sounds.

Still, a deep sadness filled her. Feeling something missing from her heart, she remembered the sodality pin with the blue ribbon floating in the air as it descended to the river. What would she do with that empty place over her heart? Or was it her heart that was empty?

Opening the porch door, which closed when she opened it

and opened when she closed it, she looked for her sodality's sheet of membership rules and principles. There it was atop the lace cloth on the dining room table. "Each bead of a rosary represents a crown of roses woven in Mary's honor," she read. Then she read again how women of "*słowackiego* (Slovak), *czeskiego* (Czech), *rusinskiego* (Ruthenian), or *litewskiego* (Lithuanian) extraction" could join the sodality. Still shaky, she couldn't read more. She felt certain she'd fix Blessed Mary's feet in heaven someday for having been through all this on earth. After seeing those delicate feet crushing the head of serpents so often on statues and in pictures, she knew the Virgin's tired feet would need skilled attention. Stella Pilsudski was the podiatrist for Blessed Mary! EXPERIENCED FOOT CARE, she'd advertise in heaven.

Mrs. Pilsudski expected the upstairs to be a mess after the long freight train's passage, Mary and Joseph fallen from the dresser, St. Anthony from the cedar chest. When she went upstairs, though, she found the saints abiding in her absence as she'd left them. Despite her wobbling legs, she kissed each saint, then kissed the feet of the Savior on the cross. Around her fingers she strung the rosary beads, wishing she could keep her hands forever steady with the rosary, steady the way her mind was now that she'd survived the ordeal on the trestle.

Looking out at the darkening river, she closed her window shades to change out of her dress, girdle, stockings. Surely Jesus could forgive a faithful woman's incontinence.

Next she washed up, studying her face in the bathroom mirror. A wrinkled face, but pink like a rose. She let the loosened knot of gray hair fall to her shoulders. Ready for bed, she sat in the wing chair—first, to praise God, then to thank Him for her blameless life. She next sought a blessing on the house, thinking how each room had stood up courageously over the years to the violent surprises of a life near the tracks. "A good house, too," whispered Pani Pilsudski, thinking of this bedroom, of the adjoining very holy and sacred bathroom, of the holy spare room down the hall. Then she thought of the living room below her with the flex-steel hide-a-bed and reupholstered chairs, holy as well; then of the holy kitchen, bright and airy with the good counter space, stainless steel sink, oven, stove, the dependable, holy, frost-free refrigerator. She prayed for her rooms, her knick-knacks, her loofah brush—all precious because she'd worked hard to acquire them. And she was the holy woman at their center, a truly holy woman radiating goodness and humility.

Next she prayed for the salmon patties in the refrigerator, for the ham and bean soup, for the half-eaten wienie bought from Jadzia's store. She prayed for herself, too, and for her dear, deceased husband, Stasiu, but mainly for herself, beseeching Jesus to allow her to keep on with Blessed Footcare Work. In fact, once the 9:17 freight passed through tomorrow morning, during the hour she could stand up without the house shaking apart, she'd clean the leftovers out of the refrigerator, then, before the next freight came through, hurry across the trestle, first to confession in the new confessional, then to buy a pound of ground chuck or a soup bone at the market. Once there, she, Stella, would drop a quarter into the March of Dimes canister—no, make that thirty cents, she thought.

Tomorrow a new and improved Pani Pilsudski, the once-lowly podiatrist who'd suffered such a great, fearsome shock at the sodality and on the trestle, would set out on a real, epic March of Dimes. No matter how long it took, she'd locate "Jerry's Kids" and make everything up to them. She'd donate to Community Chest, donate to Salvation Army, to Goodwill, even to the Volunteer Fire Department out in the country. By giving dimes and nickels from her coin purse to the very neediest of Douglas County, she'd show the world the real meaning of Christ's holy work on earth.

For now, though, pure and honest of heart again, she'd focus her attention on a good night's sleep among Jesus and His Saints. She had to admit, if anyone belonged here, she did. Pulling back the blankets, she climbed into bed, resting her head on two, rich pillows. In less than a minute, she was deeply asleep dreaming that the Holy Mother whispered to her, "Mrs. Pilsudski, you are forgiven."

Winter Weeds

I CANNOT RESIST Ewa Zukowski. When she comes to church, I push back the confessional curtain to see her bowing forward in the pew. The worship of Old Country women is hard, physical. Ewa, being grateful to God, touches her forehead to the back of the pew before her, striking her breast three times in supplication to the Lord.

Into the late afternoon, she waits 'til others leave so we can be alone. Are her sins so great that no one else can be here but she and I? Other parishioners sin deeply. Pani Stefaniak confesses to reading forbidden books and consulting fortune-tellers. Mr. Sloboda to lycanthropy: "the assumption of the form and characteristics of a wolf held to be possible by witchcraft and magic." I've heard him snarl a time or two during confession when I asked him if he had absented himself without due cause from Mass on Sundays. Another parishioner has narcolepsy. He sins, then falls asleep during confession. When I wake him, he's forgotten what he's come here for. But weeds in a bed, like Ewa Zukowski's? Her whispered confessions disturb me—her sins are a bouquet, a secret message brought to a priest in the prime of his life in this bustling Wisconsin town. In the failing light when shadows pass the baptismal font and my housekeeper, Lulu, has supper waiting, I hear Ewa clear her throat in the confessional. Through the cloth screen, she whispers, "Weeds," to me.

"What?"

"I feel them reach up my legs. My bedsheets grow weeds that yell when I yank them out. *Kurzyślep,*" she says in Polish.

"That's chickweed."

"Yes, and field and sow thistle."

"At the time of your next confession, bring them to me," I tell her.

"I'll pull one right from my pillow, Father."

"Go then and sin no more, Ewa," I say, observing her shadowy outline as she blesses herself before leaving.

The next Saturday she brings weeds to the church in a cloth bag. Calling them *Sporysz mleczny* and *Ziele sw.-janskie,* she remembers how they grew in the Old Country.

"What sins do *these* indicate?" I ask, but she will not tell me, will not whisper the answer to me. She leaves them on the railing in the confessional for the next penitent, the lycanthropic Sloboda, to froth and snarl over. He, too, leaves them there. Some of the weeds have stems with leaves and clusters of faded yellow flowers. Closing the confessional door, I genuflect at the main altar, bow at the side altar, and, with Ewa Zukowski's bouquet of weeds pressed to my heart, come through the sacristy into the rectory that adjoins the church.

"These are troublesome pasture weeds," says my housekeeper when I show her, though I don't tell her where I got them. "Old-time talismans against thunder, witches, weak eyes," she says.

"I'll put them in a vase in the front room," I say.

An hour later I hear the brittle weeds groaning. Will they be louder the next time Ewa pulls them from her sheets? A thistle with beautiful wine-red flower heads, this weed I imagine to represent Ewa's passion, Ewa tossing in a weed-choked bed at midnight, calling for her priest. Another, because it grows in open fields and waste places, because its seedlike fruits become wind-borne, and because, as I have read, its leaves "may turn on edge and become oriented like a compass in an east–west direction," this one I imagine to be a weed, not of *her* sin, but of her being sinned against.

With the weak prickles of her "compass" plant pressed to my bare chest, I divulge to my daybook what I imagine she did not say to me in confession. I tempt myself by entering into sinful reflection. I enjoy myself thinking, *Ewa, Ewa, first you went through the Nazi-occupied Sudetenland. With nothing left to you but ragged clothes and memories of your husband, who stayed in Poland to fight with the Home Army, you traded what you had for a bowl of horse-meat soup to eat. In Hungary you had to pay with your body to get food. Blessed be God that you kept your faith.*

"But I have lovely memories, too," she tells me one afternoon as children's voices come in through the windows. "I walked much of the way from Poland or rode in wagons. Two months of darkness, and Budapest was bright. People sat in outdoor cafes watching ice skaters on the Danube. I wanted blue skates," she confesses, then tells me how she got to England, then here. "My husband is coming to America," she says.

By recalling what she tells me, then transcribing it into my daybook for my own pleasure, I sin against the sacerdotal office. Before I began writing in the daybook, I was Christ's holy representative here on earth. Now the weed withers at my chest when I divulge her secrets, writing them in English because few parishioners read this language well enough to understand my thoughts and pleasures. I tell you I am a passionate man—that it is 1948, when our docks are shipping near-record tons of iron

ore, when an oil refinery (the only one in the state) will soon be
built in the East End, and when an airport is on the drawing
board for this most progressive city. We're Superior, after all. Our
motto is: SUPERIOR, WISCONSIN—ONE GREAT LAKE AND A WHOLE
LOT MORE! We live up to our name.

From her house to the church rectory is two miles. She
walks over a trestle, then west to St. Adalbert's and to me, Father
Marciniak. In winter she hikes along the river. In a spot below
the toboggan hill, city workers with wooden hand plows keep
the river snow-free for the ice skaters. Everyone knows her.
From a distance—from the edge of the ore dock—you might
think she is older than her twenty-seven years. Frost forms on
her gray overcoat; it rimes the wool scarf; but when, close up,
you notice her rosy skin pink about the cheeks from the wind,
when you notice her gaze, the firm, straight nose, the rich pale
mouth, you will soon see she is a youthful countess.

Another path she takes to me passes the general-purpose
docks that ship slag and road salt. She crosses the highway bridge
by the ore dock. The dock's pier extends into the bay. An earth
incline built on the right-of-way rises slowly out of empty fields
a mile back, then onto a dock of crossed beams and steel sup-
ports that climb eighty feet. Above the houses and stores and out
over the bay rumble ore trains, raining cinders on the neighborhood. Even from far off you hear ore sliding from the train cars
into the ore pockets, then into the lowered chutes and into iron
boats that carry their cargo to blast furnaces in Conneaut and
Buffalo. When Ewa confesses on a Saturday, we hear the ore in
the chutes.

The Martyrdom of Pinpricks says:

To manifest temptations in confession is an act of
humility which is sometimes more difficult and painful
than is the telling of a serious sin. Such a manifestation
is an act of humility. It seems that God is pleased at

times to bestow an immediate reward for such humility
by granting a prompt removal of the temptation that
was thus made known.

If true, then why do I persist in such folly as writing of my
lust for Ewa in my daybook? Why do I not myself "manifest my
temptations" to a priest in confession? Maybe to the priests at St.
Stanislaus or at Sts. Cyril and Methodius? "Sin no more," I tell
Ewa when she makes her weekly confession. Then I tell myself,
"No more sinning yourself, Father Marciniak. End this foolishness." Yet sin I will. Kneeling on the very kneeler where Ewa
knelt, its sharp wooden edge cutting my knees, I utter her words
from moments before, that she loves her husband, Grzegórż, and
patiently waits for him. Alone, I seek thoughts she has begun. I
seek the muffled sighs, evidence to let me know that I, a sinning
Marciniak, might also be desired by Ewa Zukowski.

Later in personal papers, I write on November 7, 1948:

> To the Parishioners of St. Adalbert's—
>
> If you someday come upon this among my effects,
> how will you read it, as it is written in English?
>
> "Bless me, Father," Ewa said to me. (I waited hours
> for her voice this afternoon. Church was dark, worship-
> pers having left, my supper waiting—then her gentle
> breath like wine.) "Bless me, Father Marciniak, I have
> sinned. . . ."
>
> "How? Weed sins again?"
>
> "The weed of pride appears with a hairless stem and
> coarsely toothed leaves."
>
> "Why this pride? Answer me. Are you a descendant
> of an ancient family? Is it from this your pride comes?"
>
> "No," she said.
>
> "Are you exceptionally learned?"
>
> "No."

"Rich?"

"Oh no."

"Then you're very religious or you possess great beauty and charm?"

"No, Father."

To me you do. Oh, your beauty, I think. In the votive candles' flicker, Ewa made her Act of Contrition. Seeing her head bowed against the confessional screen, I brought mine close, stealthily, so that she could not know I touched the screen or felt the sin deep in my heart.

This is as far as I wrote.

That night when Lulu cleared the dishes and went to visit the nuns across the street, I wrote to My Almighty Father. With trembling hands, I recorded how Ewa covers her face with her hands in the pew. She cannot notice me behind the confessional curtain, smothering my sighs as I wait for her. In the daybook, I wrote this word in pencil, highlighting it with red ink: "*pożądanie,* lust."

I know God permits His representative on earth this persecution. "Sufferings, contradictions, humiliations are among the greatest gifts given our souls during their earthly sojourns," says *The Martyrdom of Pinpricks.*

That night, I wrote more:

Dearest Pan Lord Jezu,

Forgive in me the pull of the flesh. I take you as my Sole Ruler. When Ewa left church today, I sought by candlelight a hair of hers that I hoped had caught in the confessional screen as a golden thread might from your garment, Dear Lord. I placed my lips where hers whispered. Her red lips . . . I will soon enough touch them at Communion. . . .

Later, unable to sleep with the temptation of it, I cried, "*Wierze w Boga Ojca,*" asking God's forgiveness. Imploring Him, I called out so loudly in the church rectory at midnight that Lulu came in bewildered at being awakened.

"Do you need a doctor? Is that it?" Lulu asked. "What kind of priest cries like this?"

Out of joy and grief, I said, "I know she loves me."

"What?" said Lulu, shocked. "Are you lycanthropic? Are you a werewolf like Sloboda?"

"The Virgin, God's Mother, loves me."

"Oh," she said, suspicious.

• • •

I see after Mass in the morning (November 8, the Feast of the Four Holy Crowned Martyrs) that you, Ewa, have placed an ad in our daily paper, the *Dziennik:*

> Woman desires to do old-style cooking for you. Has
> much experience. Telephone "Ewa" at Export 8-5552.

My chance to sample her cooking comes when Lulu goes to Duluth to Petrolle's Altar Goods Store. "Take the day off," I tell Lulu. "Get away for awhile. Here's bus fare."

I pay Ewa to prepare *bigos,* a hearty hunter's stew. I need my strength for the Advent season. As we talk in the kitchen, she tells me she is getting her cooking and baking business started so she will have money when her husband arrives. When I hand her the pepper, she thinks the touch of my hand is accidental.

"I can write the recipe down for you if you'd like me to," she says.

"Yes. Write it here. Please don't turn the pages, however. This is my secret book."

"A priest's secrets? What are your secrets?"

"They involve . . . what is the weed of impurity?"

"*Werwena* or *Koszysko lekarskie,*" she says.

"What does *werwena* look like? I've only heard of it, though of course I myself have felt no lust or impurity."

"It's full of soft hairs. It grows in my bed. I will pull one out for you or sweep one from my floor."

"How do you recognize it, Ewa? I'm a priest and have to know. Show me."

"You recognize it by its waving, silken hairs."

Before she leaves after cooking, she allows me to kiss her cheek. When I can no longer see her from my upstairs window, I run to open the daybook where she's written, "Cut up any meat that you may have left over. Brown a spoonful of butter, add some meat (pork, beef, venison, sausage) or vegetable stock, a few diced apples, some onion, if desired, then the sauerkraut and a lump of sugar. Simmer gently until the *bigos* is done."

Under a microscope the next day I study the strand of her hair from the confessional. I write in my book about the curve of her neck, where the hair grows dark, then about her eyebrows, her eyes, her deep red lips stained like currants in the Polish meadows. *At the instant I call God's name at midnight, you, Ewa, call mine. I know it and feel the weeds about my ankle. This I say truly unto you: there it is, the werwena weed with the soft hairs. Two mornings later when you receive the Eucharist, my fingertips brush your lips.*

• • •

All day and night, crews work the Northern Pacific dock. Everyone is gainfully employed. Taverns are full. Churches are full. New cars go by. The war is over.

Our hills to the south are snow covered; the Left-Handed River is frozen. Late in the shipping season—November, December—with the ore boats waiting to load and sail before the lakes freeze over, the ore dockmen, the ore punchers who want to make money, have time only for a fast meal and a hard sleep, then back to the dock. Too often, unmarried men settle for smoked sausage and sauerkraut at the Warsaw Tavern or for pigs' feet in the vat at the butcher's by the gas plant.

The men carry suppers home in waxed paper, stare at their kitchen walls, then fall into bed exhausted from "punching" ore with their long poles. Their two-story houses have brown tarpaper shingles and front porches. The upstairs rooms are closed off in winter, used for storing perishables. In the downstairs is a kitchen, a tiny living room with a cot and woodstove, and a chilly front room through whose windows these prosperous workmen can be seen in suspenders and undershirts nodding asleep or walking back and forth from room to room, back and forth in fading light.

One of the men says to me in confession, "Father, will God be angry if I spend more money on food?"

"Do you work hard? Do you pray morning and night and have plenty of overtime pay?"

"Yes. But I have no time to cook."

"Are you moderate in your other habits?"

"Yes. But I can't cook."

"A man has to eat. I think God wants you to keep your strength. You'll have someone to talk to. You're alone after work. Who will cook for you? Probably an old woman who can come after working in the hospital."

A week later, the same ore puncher confesses something terrible. He says he loves his cook.

"It's a scourge of thorns," I say. "Put away these thoughts!"

But two days later, he's back to speak of Ewa. Four days later, he comes again.

I know that this ore puncher tithes his ten percent, drinks moderately, has never married. At age thirty-four or thirty-five, he works hard and wears an odd coat. Purchased from a religious guild, it has a broken heart sewn on the back.

So, I think, my beautiful parishioner Ewa, for whom I lust,

has been coming to me in a state of mortal sin these mornings. Standing before her, in my hands the ciborium, myself quite sick for love of her and for Jesus, I cannot turn away from her. "May the Body of Our Lord preserve your soul unto life everlasting," I say, laying the Blessed Host upon her tongue. Even unto God's altar she will come in sin. One morning she leaves me the *wer-wena,* the lust weed, right on the altar railing. With the candles extinguished, the water and wine put away, the acolytes gone home, she remains to pray before the Virgin's statue. Seeing her, I can't calm myself. I stand in my alb and cincture. The cincture, the cord that girds the alb when a priest dresses for Mass, symbolizes the chastity and continence required of me.

"Am I not a good man, too?" I say aloud. "Am I not scourged? Have I not suffered? I understand the weaknesses of the body as well as any man and as well as you, Ewa. I knew when you exhibited exterior restlessness that the devil was working," I tell her. "I thought your restlessness was only for me."

I approach her. I try holding her, try kissing her hand and cheek the way I did in the kitchen.

"I'm lonely without my husband. There's no hope for me," she whispers.

"Untie the cord," I say to her. Frightened, she whispers again that all is hopeless.

"Untie the symbol of chastity. That's it. Loose me from it, Ewa. Join me in loneliness."

All through the remainder of that Sunday, I wear my cincture tightened again. I write in my daybook:

> Dearest God,
> I come to you in humble contrition. Despite the
> guidance of Your Church, Ewa cannot release herself
> from despair. Each Saturday she confesses that she—

Oh, her sins humiliate me, yet I make her repeat them.
It brings sad pleasure to a priest.

"What do you do with him? When you are alone,
where does he put his hands? Where does he particular-
ly touch you? Does he put his tongue there? Does he
grasp you from behind?" These are the things I ask.

One afternoon Stanislaus Coda weeps in front of me. Have *I*
not wept for his and Ewa's hopeless souls? In *The Soul's Combat,*
Blessed Peter Faber teaches that God allows a bad man (Stanislaus Coda) to wrong a good man (Father Marciniak) in order
that the immense power of the forgiving prayer of the good man
(Father Marciniak) may win the grace needed by the bad man,
who else must perish. Just when I thought I'd saved Stanislaus
Coda, however, he told me he'd stopped eating.

"Father, a fast will help me," he says.

Though pierced by the news of his sins with Ewa, I am *certain* no one is in the other side of the confessional.

"I don't know what to do to avoid sin, Father. I have nothing
else in life."

"Think of hers, this woman's, soul as well as your own,
Stanislaus, the double sin of adultery."

"I'm trying to improve by starving. How do holy men such
as you, Father . . . are you ever tempted this way?"

"Never! Not by impurity. I'd sooner jump from the ore
dock."

"I should jump from the ore dock then?" asks Coda.

"I don't know. Let me think. Kneel awhile longer," I say as I
pretend to pray.

*I know how it's happened. He's opened a heat vent to a room. Then
he's come back downstairs. As she, a married woman, makes soup, he
throws wood into the stove. As she, the wife of Korporał Grzegórz*

Zukowski, tends the frying pan, Stanislaus takes up stirring the beets. As she slides the bread from the oven and slices the butter, he checks over the table. Hovering about in his gray shirt, wool pants, and heavy shoes, he wipes his nervous hands on his pants, takes a drink, then says to her, "Ewa darling." Dear God, I thought the werwena weeds grown in lust-ful thoughts and dreams and found in her bed were for me alone. This is a moment, a grain of sand in an eternity that cannot end. This is one long moment in an eternity of love.*

"That you permit yourself earthly pleasures is scandalous," I tell Coda. "This woman is failing you. You must honor the Commandment regarding venery before it's too late and her husband returns to her. The following are signs by which the soul will know whether it is finally detached from the pleasures of the senses: If the exercises of the spirit be the soul's chief delight and are pursued diligently, if . . ." *I do not hear anyone enter the other side of the confessional. She must have followed him to church.* "If you seek not after nor willingly read profane literature, if you do not encourage particular friendships, modern improvements, the telephone . . ." *She must have blessed herself before entering the sacred residency of the confessional. I can hear her kneel. I am busy instructing the sinner.* "We've small reason to love our bodies, Stanislaus. They're the cause of all sin. To satisfy their cravings . . ."

"When she makes my supper, Father, I look at her and must touch her."

"St. John Chrysostom tells us, it's not lawful to say 'I cannot resist sin,' for that means accusing the Creator. You should leap from the dock. You have to end this. 'Out of the depths, I cry to you, O Lord . . .'"

She is in the other side. As Stanislaus prays, I hear her whispering, "I've doubted six times. I've done unnecessary servile work on Sundays and Holy Days. I've committed adultery. I've cheated in prices and weights . . . have injured others' reputations. In the bend of my shoulder lies Stanislaus's head when we're naked. I wear the loose blouse to entice him. His body joins mine," she is saying. "I've let a priest kiss me to show me the powerful intercession of God's love—"

"Stop it, Ewa!" I whisper. "Don't bring scandal to him or me."

"I've been to the priest's, have let him kiss me. Worse than that, he—"

As Ewa and Coda confess to me, I pray aloud, "He came unto His own and His own received Him not. Your anointed flesh, Ewa."

"I desire her," Coda says.

"I've been with a priest," Ewa says. "Husband Grzegórż is traveling to me in America."

Through the woven screens, both sides confessing. . . .

Then *I* say, "To as many as received Him He gave the power of becoming sons of God," while Coda mutters, "No, not *you* in sin, Ewa."

"Injured reputations. Cheating in prices and weights. Doing servile work on Sundays," Ewa says.

"Out of my heart comes impurity," I say. "Your holy flesh, Ewa."

When Stanislaus beats his fists against the confessional wall, I clutch my rosary, huddle in the booth. When Stanislaus runs out of church, I give the Lord thanks for my safety.

This is a shipping season in an afternoon in eternity. We have a long, long time to go: A grain of sand is a million years; two grains, two million years; four grains, four million years.

He returns an hour later. I cower in the confessional booth. Stanislaus Coda needs to say an Act of Contrition. Mr. Dulinski, the narcoleptic, is asleep in his pew. I hear a vicious snarl outside. It is the lycanthropic Sloboda. Then comes Stanislaus, who says he has repented. Strangely, he says he isn't hungry. I tell him all sins are forgiven. Because of confession, his hunger has been taken away. "*Ego te absolvo,*" I repeat.

"I'm absolved?"

"Yes, though try to do better."

From then on, I learn he eats unappetizing meals of his own making. Though Stanislaus perhaps has a little more time for stewed duck or carp with sauce on Sundays, he has no appetite, Ewa tells me. The few times she's dared to go to him, he's banked snow around the house. "Come in," he's said grudgingly. His heat vents are closed. When she enters his house, she tells me three candles flicker where he has them on a kitchen cabinet. In a blue workshirt, he sits, elbows on the table, thinking, staring at the coat hanging on the wall. He tells her he sleeps at the table with his coat on. He doesn't want any meals from her, he says. He gives her the coat one day. A moth-eaten coat with the heart on the back, it is too large for her. "Has your husband come from Poland yet?" he asks her.

Ewa, too, stops eating—on December 10, when we honor St. Melchiades. I, on the other hand, am ravenous for potato pancakes and for *zając pieczony,* the rabbit Ewa once made to perfection. Lulu, my housekeeper, never gets rabbit right. When I say, "You didn't use enough flour," she shakes her head and replies, "Wiser the egg than the hen." I give her a new recipe for rabbit, one that requires Lulu to dredge the rabbit in flour three or four times more than she has been. Included in the recipe are chopped mushrooms, one chopped onion, pinches of dry thyme, bay leaves, a cup of tart white wine. She is to cut the rabbit into desired pieces, dredging and dredging it in the flour and browning it in butter, then baking until tender. She says, "*Głod wilka z lasu wyprowadzi* . . . Hunger will lead a fox out of the forest."

She keeps me alive so I can suffer. You'll see that no prolonged death by starvation appears in these pages of my day-book. If spiritual remorse is knowing we can never share God's company in heaven, then Ewa Zukowski, whom Stanislaus Coda and I place before God Himself, makes earthly existence a pur-gatory. I wish the priest Marciniak, the ore puncher Coda, and the beautiful Ewa could be stricken from this book of life. Death never visits and never will, and now her husband is coming. We live a long, dark, joyless life, only we three, while the rest of the neighborhood prospers. Our grievous sins and the knowledge of them separate us. We do not prosper. We both touched Ewa, Stanislaus and I. That day in confession it was as if I myself had watched them fornicate. I've cried out loud, "I will keep on my cincture." I've told this to the Lord. How I wish she'd eat, though. Weeks later, she looks ghostlike. Seeing her, the nuns and I shake our heads after the Low Mass.

I give Lulu a recipe for meatloaf filled with buckwheat groats. I stay alive on leftovers, even on Sunday. Eating enough for any man, I grow neither faint nor weak, though I do not eat what I like.

I see Stanislaus Coda walking up on the Northern Pacific dock when he's not working. If the wind blinds us these December afternoons, you can imagine how dangerous things are up there for the man who doesn't eat. In such a perilous state, a soul should seek comfort through the continual renewal of confession and absolution administered by His holy represen-tative on earth. If not confession and absolution from me, then from another priest.

Ewa cooks for other people, though not for Stanislaus Coda, who has now gone on a long fast. Each morning he eats a crust of bread. I eat Lulu's meals, but I am never satisfied. Ewa doesn't eat at all, but she doesn't die. Life is a mystery. I accept it on faith. Coda just walks back and forth high up on the ore dock. For

Ewa's penance, I make her go down there each day. Eighty feet above her, she might sometimes see the starving Coda, though you couldn't be certain it was him with the ore cars and steam locomotives all over up there and the men steering the ore through the open chutes into the boats. The rods Coda and the boys swing to start the ore flowing weigh twenty pounds and are five feet long. Try freezing in the cold staring upward for eight hours, hoping to find heaven in the man you love. Try crouching beneath an ore car, punching ore all day. Weak as you are, you'll get hungry and sick of your adulterous life.

For my penance, for the priest Father Julius Marciniak's penance, I gather weeds from the frozen earth of East End. Lulu finds them in my coat pockets, finds them beneath my pillows, finds them all over my sheets. I think Lulu, my housekeeper, is in love with me. The weeds of sin groan when she pulls them. During the eternity of winter, when weeds grow from ice and snow, we are all very hungry, Lulu included, hungry and unsatisfied, but I keep thinking hunger will lead the fox out of the forest.

Closing Time

WHY HIRE BUCK MROZEK? Because I, Buck, am talented. I am husband, parent, wage earner, dependable officer in the Polish Club of Superior, Wisconsin. My grown kid Rick has written me a letter saying he's going to join. During one Polish Club membership drive, I signed up a Terry O'Connor, who was asleep at the bar. We'd never seen him here. If you're not Polish or are over forty-five, you can only be a "social member" and cannot vote on lodge matters. Also, according to Article 1 of our Polish Club Constitution and By-Laws, to swear someone in, two active lodge members must be present. Al Wojciech woke this Mr. O'Connor, Soapy Zileski raised the candidate's hand, and I read him the oath for new members.

Then a year later comes a letter stamped in red on the outside:

Inmate Correspondence
Chillicothe Correctional Inst.
Chillicothe, OH 45601

On a sheet of legal paper, social member O'Connor wrote:

Hi, Polish Club

I'd like to resien the Polish Club. I no longer want
to be a member. I'm not Polish, and I never will be &
and I won't marry a Polish person nor will my family.
So Drop me & my family from the Roles of the Polish.
Didn't the Catholics kill Lord Jesus Christ. I'm not a
Catholic & never will be or my family.

I'm not a Pope lover, ever forever. The Pope's a Polish ain't he? I'm free of you Catholics forever. Amen.
I'm a Lutheran forever amen! Terry O'Connor PS. Take
my name off of your mailing list! I joined when I was
drunk. Be humbel!

We took some ribbing for signing up a drunk who later
landed in prison. Still, I can count on one hand the other mistakes I've made in twenty years. One was falling away from the
Church, which I am thankful to my wife I'm back in now.
Another mistake was not going to see the Holy Father, Pope
John Paul II, when he was in Des Moines. Others were not
meeting Frankie Yankovic, who's now a Grammy Award winner;
not bumping up to a better job on the packing floor at the flour
mill when I had the chance; and never going to Poland to see
where my ancestors came from. However, these are good reasons
to hire me, because I, Buck Mrozek, composer and performer of
polkas, have lived, loved, and made mistakes, all of which trans-
lates into passionate polka playing. Do you think my line of
work is easy with kids all the time listening to Boy George and
Prince's "When Doves Cry"? The good music is crowded off the
airwaves of the Northland, or old-timers are sick and can't get
out to hear it anymore. But there's nothing like polka for good
times and high spirits. Though in some places doors slam shut
and laughter explodes at the mere mention of polka, I'm a polka
crusader, which I've given my life to and still do.

Why hire Buck Mrozek, solo artist? Because I'm dependable and am free to play weekends. I just need time to wash up. Helen will have supper and a clean shirt waiting, so all I have to do is grab the sheet music and the accordion case, and I'm out the door. I will travel locally to halls in Duluth-Superior, Cloquet, Moose Lake, Barnum, Wrenshall, Carlton, Poplar—though Poplar, Wisconsin, is getting close to Oulu Hotshots territory. They are a good band, the Hotshots, who I respect and who play at the Little Kro-Bar in Brule.

Part of my sincere belief is that you should help when some member of a band is out sick or for personal reasons. I'd work with the Hotshots or with the Chmielewski Fun-Time Band of Sturgeon Lake, Minnesota, if they called on me, which they never do. If I started a band like my old one, we'd never get bookings, because there are already the Hotshots and Chmielewskis for hire, as well as a few solo performers like myself. But the main reason is that there's little call for the polka entertainer in today's society. So I go it alone, playing from eight to eleven one night a month in the bar of the VFW, always trying to make the case for polka. "The best help is self-help," says a Polish proverb.

This was what my new German lady-friend must've been thinking, too, when she requested "Westphalia." Her husband was talking to people. I was playing "Helena Polka." She walks over with her request on a slip of paper, which she set down in front of me and I nodded at her. As I played, I watched. After a lifetime in the army and a lifetime of being married to her, her husband didn't notice his Frau Gusti crying over what I was playing. When I began "Edelweiss," she was so heartbroken she left for the ladies' room.

Knowing how sadness hits us—and to even things out for that crying lady—I played a number that broke my own heart. "Come back, Blue Lady, come back," I sang. When she returned from the ladies', I had tears in my eyes for the associations the beautiful "Blue Skirt Waltz" recalls. Every one of my polkas, obereks, and waltzes brings sorrow and joy to me. With that one, I remember my boy, Ricky, when I was in the kitchen practicing. I always kept the door open between the kitchen and the living room when I played. I was in no mood for any lip when he shut the door on my accordion stylings.

"Leave 'er open while I practice 'Blue Skirt Waltz.'"

"I can't hear the show on TV I'm watching, Pa," he said.

"Fine and dandy, but leave the kitchen door open, Ricky," I said, wanting him—wanting *somebody!*—to hear my life in my music. *Listen for it, Ricky—Dad's heart in this music he plays.*

When he shrugged, slouching back into the living room, I started "American Patrol" with extra feeling to inspire him. My daughter was outside, Helen was on the phone upstairs talking to her sister Ceil, but Ricky listened to his dad—or so I thought until a half-hour later when I put away the accordion. That's when I found the TV off and the living room empty. He'd gone up to his bedroom, hadn't heard me practice at all. When I went to his room looking for him, he had cotton in his ears and had piled dirty laundry over the warm air vent to block out the sound of my music. This hurts me. *Listen for Dad's heart in his music, Ricky.*

Probably it also hurt Frau Gusti Swapinski when her husband talked to everyone at the bar but her. Then, to worsen things, when he got half-a-bun on and started singing, "*In München steht ein Hofbräuhaus . . .* The man goes in and the man comes out—DRUNK!" he wouldn't let *her* join in. It was as if Spec. 7 Ray Swapinski, retired, loved her in Deutschland when he was stationed there, but after two kids with her in America, he hated who he'd brought home to the U.S. in 1950, and now it was 1983 and there was his *Frau* beside him inhibiting his fun as she had throughout their married life. He kept singing louder, "*In München steht ein Hofbräuhaus*" and got people near him to clink their beer glasses together, but threatening looks from him kept Gusti's glass quiet.

A month later, it's June, and Ray and Gusti are here again. The post commander, Bart Coplac, sets up my card table in the corner. There are twenty-seven stools at the long bar in the narrow room, plus eight small tables with chairs and stools at each. When I get ready to perform, I slide a thin strip of fiberboard into a slot milled into a foot-long piece of three-quarter-inch-round molding. This serves as my music stand. Stacking sheet music on the table, I unfasten the case, pull out the accordion, slip my tired arms through accordion straps, unsnap the bellows, signal the bartender to bring my 7-Up, then I test the mike and play "Clarinet Polka," which serious polkaholics know is the popular name of "*Dziadunia* Polka . . . Grandfather Polka." For Bolesław "Buck" Mrozek, age sixty-three, my VFW night is the high point of a month, except for Sunday Mass, honoring the Holy Days of Obligation when they come, and taking Helen to Eddie's Supper Club for the hand-breaded chicken.

Though Post 435 is noisy, people sometimes listen and dance, because I'm a high-ranking official of polkadom. If the great Frankie Yankovic (though he plays in the Slovenian not the Polish style) is our Commander-in-Polka-Chief and if people like Li'l Wally, Stas Golonka, Scrubby Seweryniak, and Eddie Blazonczyk are four-star generals in the cavalcade of polka players, then after all these years I am at least a captain. I know schottisches and songs of different nations. Your Scandinavian likes "Johann Pa Snippen" and "Nikolina's Butterfly," your German ladies like Gusti like "Lili Marlene," your Mexican enjoys "Peanut Polka," your Slovak "Tinker Polka."

I'm playing "Lili Marlene" tonight, which is the third or

fourth time I've ever seen Gusti, while Ray is yakking away. She's in this snug dress, flat shoes, and looks nice though thin, a little stoop-shouldered because she's trying to hide her height, but still is pretty for being my age or older. Who am I, Buck, to talk about appearances, being in the terminal stage of male-pattern baldness and missing a front tooth, which I wear a partial for? Playing the accordion at my bandstand in the far back corner by the bathrooms, I look up front at the mannequins in the entry-way, each dressed in a different armed services uniform. Then I see her sad look, as if hearing me play she misses her homeland. She's out of place and doesn't say much to Ray's crowd. No mat-ter how she tries, her quietness plus her being taller than every-body and being born outside the United States make her differ-ent from the ladies native to Superior.

As accordionist-in-residence, I get lonely, too. The kids are grown, Helen is a stay-at-home wife, and I am playing in what seems like the last outpost on earth for polkas and old standards. I'm background music to everyone but Ray's wife.

What got me about my kids—Lorraine, the daughter, as well as Ricky—was they ridiculed my music. I think about them as I play, and Ray is getting drunk. Now that the kids are older, they're coming around to my way of thinking. Ricky lives in North Tonawanda, New York, a fine Polish area, plenty of bands, lots of music on radio. Lorraine teaches history at a Jesuit college in Wheeling, West Virginia. On the radio she pulls in the polka shows from Pittsburgh. I remember when we had the wall phone hanging in the pantry, Lorraine's college teacher called. He wanted her to proctor an exam for him. She cupped her hand over the phone, tried to muffle the music as I practiced. When her conversation ended, she hung up and started in on me, "Do you know how embarrassed I am right now, Dad? That was Dr. Feldman, my history professor!" When she calmed her-

self, she took a long bath. When I tapped on the bathroom door
next to the kitchen, asking, "Can I serenade you with something
through the door before I quit for the night, Lorraine?" she
flushed the toilet. She didn't know (Ricky didn't know either)
that I was trying to keep Old World culture alive in this country.
They can't know what they will lose until the music finally
stops. Gusti, I believe, knows, judging from how she sits quietly
beside her husband without smiling.

When I take my break, Ray, the bigmouth wearing a sports
shirt and khaki pants, comes down to my end. He's got dainty,
knobby legs I remember from seeing him in shorts, but a huge
chest that looks like it could bump you if you disobeyed him.
He's risen pretty far up the enlisted ranks, having been in the
army so long.

He stuffs a dollar-fifty into my shirt pocket, says, "Keep playing, *Polaki*. Don't quit. Don't let the mood change. What're you
resting at the bar for?"

"I wish I was Frankie Yankovic," I say.

"You'd be a richer man," he says. "But you're okay with a
squeezebox. Keep playing. Get up on that stage," by which he
means I should go back to my card table and music stand. He
acts as if people must listen to him, even though men in this bar
have fought at the Chosin Reservoir and on Iwo Jima. A World
War I vet even stops in now and then.

But Buck can take orders, which is another reason I should
be hired for dances and parties. I immediately obey Spec. 7
Swapinski's command as he stumbles off. As I start my set with
"Iron Range Polka," we hear a crash and clanging coming from
the men's room, then a thud. Bart Coplac and the bartender rush
past, then Gusti and the customers, so I'm last to see the metal
towel dispenser ripped from the men's room wall and Ray,
drunker than we thought, lying on the tile floor, fifteen feet of

cloth wound about his arms from pulling at the towel dispenser.

"*Gott im Himmel!*" Gusti cries.

Under the harsh fluorescent lights, Ray Swapinski gets more coiled up in the towel with each frenzied move.

"I want some fried shrimps," he mumbles as they help him unwind himself.

"You're going home right now," his wife says.

To keep people's minds off of Ray's accident and out of decency to a vet, I play a lively *krakowiak,* from which it is thought the polka evolved.

"I didn't think he was drunk," says the bartender.

"Sarge, you're gonna be okay," says the post commander to Ray, who's unwinding the last foot of towel from his arm.

"This thing attacked me," Ray mutters. He kicks the dispenser, then, managing to stand, does a clumsy *krakowiak.*

"Please, Ray, come home," says Gusti.

He says "Get away!" in a flash of anger you could see he reserved only for his wife. Judging from the way his face contorts so that it is almost blue, I think to myself, such anger directed against too many people would kill a man.

"Stop that music!" he says angrily to me. This time I refuse his order. As I resume my position at the card table, finishing the *krakowiak* as I go, I recall from my own military days the second General Order: "To walk my post in a military manner, keeping always on the alert and observing everything that takes place within sight or hearing." After observing Ray getting everyone riled, I think we need a bouncy tune, "Tiny Bubbles."

When he finally comes out of the men's room, disoriented, he salutes *me,* Buck Mrozek.

I nod at him the way I do when Gusti makes requests, another kind of which she's making now, requesting her husband to hand over the car keys so she can drive him home.

"*I* give orders, Gusti. I'm Ray Swapinski," he says.

"I'm not going anywhere with you drunk, Ray. You don't need fried shrimp," Gusti says.

Before I finish "Tiny Bubbles," Gusti is sitting by herself, and I can't tell if she's crying again. It saddens me to see such quarreling in the world. Then I realize how far *I* am from home at ten o'clock at night, that I'm old, that I miss Helen. I took our second car tonight, the Pinto, which is giving us trouble. Three miles home to the East End, and in an hour I still have to pack up the accordion, the music stand, and the sheet music, lugging them to the car so I can drive home, go to bed, get up, go to work.

It's hard being away from home and feeling your age. The back and neck stiffen. At night the eyes don't work good. You want to be home on the couch. I think it's partly in a person's mind. You realize that three miles is a long journey. A lot could happen. Someone could tailgate you. You might have to stop for gas at the M&C, which takes time when you want to get home to the wife.

"You played 'Tiny Bubbles' twice already!" someone yells from the bar.

"Oh, sorry," I say, stopping in the middle of the Don Ho classic to start a schottische. Of twenty words I know in Gusti's language, "*schottische*" means "Scottish." "*Ich liebe dich*" means "I love you," which she must've once said to her Ray here or in the Old World, though now Ray Swapinski has gone in quest of his "shrimps," and Bart Coplac is heading into the men's room with paper towels for vets who wash their hands.

I think of a funny event. Back when I was financial secretary of the Polish Club, we invited the bishop of the diocese to be an honorary lodge member. After his official swearing in, I went into the men's room. His Excellency was at the urinal. I didn't want to watch him as I waited to relieve myself. For something to do, I whistled, washed my hands at the sink. When I visited the urinal after the bishop had flushed it, he said, "That's the first time I've seen someone wash his hands *before* he peed."

"As always, you're right, Your Excellency," I said, feeling so foolish I wanted to kneel and kiss his ring, but he was headed for the bar.

After "Pennsylvania Polka," I see Gusti stare at her watch, then ask the bartender if the clock in the VFW is on standard or "bar time." No Spec. 7 Swapinski in sight this June night. How long does it take to order shrimps, to eat, to get back here? I expect the big chest to push through the door at any moment and all of us stand to salute the accomplishments of Spec. 7 Ray Swapinski, a veteran.

In anticipation of his return, I play an *oberek* and a couple of slow numbers before I see it's wrap-up time. No one notices when I snap the bellows shut after "Tick-Tock Polka" and fold the metal chair. Gusti has been nursing a Black Russian. Nothing is left of it but ice in the bottom of the glass. When I walk past her, accordion case in one hand, music stand in my other, I tell her, "If you need a ride, I will drive you, Madam Gusti."

She says, "*Danke schöen,*" then "no" as she consults her watch.

When I return to be sure that I didn't leave my sheet music and to bid good night to Barton Coplac, the bartender says, "You know where Gusti's old man went to?"

"Maybe I can't wait for him," says Gusti.

"Well, come on in my old car," I say.

Most nights, bars up and down Tower Avenue are full of college-aged to old-aged drinkers. For a city its size, twenty-seven thousand people, Superior has the highest rate of alcohol sales in the nation. When Frau Gusti and I walk out, crowds of youngsters cross the street from the Cove Cabaret to the Lamplighter to the Castaways. Down the avenue comes yelling and music from inside the bars. Police call the corner of Tower and North Sixth, where these three bars are located, the Golden Triangle. With all the partygoers—many crossing over from Duluth—the Golden Triangle means trouble for police at closing time.

"I'll get your car door, Gusti. Roll down the window if it's stuffy."

Opening my side, I realize that no woman but my own *Frau* has sat beside me in the front seat of this old Pinto while I was driving. I wonder, Do I look all right? Does the interior smell? I wish I had an air freshener.

"Whew, it's stuffy in here," I say.

"I don't know where Ray is."

"It's sure warm."

"Where could he be eating?"

"In any restaurant. You like to polka?"

"Ya," she says, pronouncing it in a different way from the rest of us.

"Is Germany nice? *Polka* is the Polish word for 'Polish woman.' I live in the East End. Where to?"

"I don't know where to. Ya, Germany's nice."

"He shouldn't leave you."

"That's Raymie," she says.

Now I realize it's the first time, not in twelve, but in *forty* years a beautiful woman has sat so close. It's always Helen in here, which satisfies me plenty. But still I am afraid to look, even to peek out of the corner of my eye at Gusti in the car.

When we turn onto Belknap Street, I say, "It's the nicest night of summer."

We pass Cathedral Junior High, where the kids went when it was still a high school, then pass Filteau Brothers Amoco. I say, "The A&W serves shrimp."

I can feel her looking at me. I'm afraid to look back. I keep telling myself it's just a ride, that she wants to look for Ray.

"Oh, *Gott!*" she says, ducking when I pull in to the A&W. Partly hidden, she peers over the inside of the car door. On the tray attached to the rolled-down, driver's side window of Ray's car stand two greasy A&W boxes next to a megaphone-shaped root beer container. Empty ketchup packets lay scattered where Ray's tossed them to the asphalt. The top of his expanded chest looks bigger than ever, as though he's about to bark an order to the carhop for more shrimps and, damn it, she better listen. He appears content—as though Gusti is far from his mind.

As I take off, she remains hidden. "You can get up now, Frau Gusti," I tell her when we pass Patti's Tailor Shop.

She's had a few more Black Russians than I figured. When she's done looking back, I say, "I'll get you home, but the light breeze is nice. It's seventy-five degrees tonight."

"He's not home yet!" she says to herself.

"I bet I can outeat him," I say.

"We have two kids."

"We do, too, Ricky and Lorraine. All that fried food and ketchup—will he get indigestion? I would. I'd like to have fried shrimp now, too."

"He can eat all right. Do you want to be like that?" she asks as if she's speaking in a dream, as though Spec. 7 Swapinski was something from the past.

"The difference, no matter what I eat, is that I'm married and wouldn't treat my wife like that."

When she says, "I'm married, too," it makes no sense, since that is why she's here, to look for her husband. I hope that perhaps as well as being a little stiff, she's nervous being with me, nervous in a good way.

"Let's just go to another drive-in," I say.

It's two miles to the Frostop. Barker's Island Marina is lit up as we drive by. Beyond it, the dark bay, Wisconsin Point with a few twinkling lights among the pines, then the vast darkness of Lake Superior. On East Second Street, moths flit about the lamps and die in the gutter. We say nothing, but I am more aware of the pleasant breeze than ever before in forty years of being married to Helen. When we pass the streetlight at 20th and East Second, I say, "Look out for Lili Marlene," wondering what I meant by it; perhaps I was trying to be smooth like a youth with a girl. "Lili Marlene" is a song about the German woman during war who waits beneath the streetlight for her American soldier.

"You said you wouldn't treat me like Ray," she says, laying her hand on my shoulder. I see that it is really not an old hand and that she has taken off her wedding ring. Suddenly neither Frau Gusti nor the King of Polka is old.

Swallowing hard, I get the strength to look at her beautiful face, the gray-blond hair in waves or curls that let you see a little of her ears.

"I am a World War II vet," I tell her.

"We all are," she says, cupping her hands in her lap.

Nervous, I say, "I better check things." Peering over my shoulder to see that the accordion case and everything are doing okay in back, I say, "Look. That's where we're going," as I point ahead to the drive-in.

"Are you hungry?" she asks.

"*Jawohl,* Frau Gusti," I say.

"Goosti, pronounce it like 'Ow-goost-a,'" she says.

"What was Germany like?"

"Occupied by men like Ray, who I had two babies with, then came to the United States."

"I was in another branch of the service for four years. Spent the rest of my career down here," I tell her, pointing through the darkness on the waterfront to the flour mill's red-neon sign a half-block below us on the bay. Even though, when I go to work each day, I pass the Frostop Drive-In, where we're now pulling in to eat, I don't think the carhop will be able to identify the man who in nine hours will trudge past again with his lunch bucket.

When the girl steps out into the harsh drive-in lights to take our orders, I tell her, "Two fish combos and two 7-Ups, hon."

"Can you roll down your window a little more when I bring your food?" she asks.

"Aren't you getting shrimp?" says Gusti.

"In terms of eating, I'm not as much like Ray as I thought," I tell her, wondering how it'd be, with Helen at home four blocks from here, knowing I'll see Helen in an hour, knowing I'll see the guys at the mill in nine hours, wondering how it would be to touch lonely Gusti's hand just once. At my age, I maybe will never be close to a beautiful woman again if I don't touch her hand.

She reads my thoughts. I see in the look on her face that she herself cannot be free, but there is tonight at least at the Frostop.

"It is the only time in a long married life I've done something like this," I tell Gusti when we untangle our fingers, letting go of each other's hands. I hope Helen will not smell the fish combos in the Pinto and grow suspicious.

"Don't you like tartar sauce?" Gusti asks, recovering her composure.

"*Nein, meine Frau*," I say, heart pounding, hands shaking when I give her the ketchup packets. Her heart is pounding, too. "I watch you when you're sitting beside Ray," I tell her. Still not believing we held hands or that she laid her gentle hand on my shoulder, I spill root beer on my shirt and wipe a dribble from my chin before she sees it.

"There's not much between Ray and me anymore."

"You're something to see, Gusti. You're really beautiful."

"Don't think I'm not listening with all my heart when you play your songs at the VFW. I remember them from during the war. You're not as old as I am," she says. "You know what I wonder, Buck . . . how you play for four straight hours without going pee."

"I can hold it in, like I am now," I tell her.

"You got Ray beat for bladder control," she says.

When we're finished eating and the carhop returns, I ask, "Could my girl and I drive around back here, look at the bay under the stars, sit on a picnic bench?" Saying it hurts me, because as much as we want to, Gusti could never be my girl. I have my beautiful wife of forty years. She has Ray, the shrimp eater.

"We're closing, but sure. Say, you work at the flour mill, don't you?" the carhop says, winking.

"I hold two jobs," I tell her. When I tip her, I give her the dollar-fifty Ray gave me. Gusti gives her another dollar, then I give the carhop a dollar "hush money," so she won't tell anyone she saw me.

"People are plenty lonely," I say to Gusti when the drive-in's lights go off, leaving only the red neon shimmering the words FREDERICKA FLOUR on the bay below. "It's nice tonight. We should get out of the car. It's a pretty sight down there. It's like I don't have to pee at all now," I say.

Both of us anticipate something. It is as if the balmy night air anticipates it, as if the green light marking the Wisconsin Point harbor entryway across the dark bay expects something on such a beautiful, romantic evening. I know Ray will either return to the VFW looking for Gusti or will give up and head home to a bed made crisp that morning by his German wife. Unlike Gusti and me tonight, he has nothing more exciting to anticipate than drive-in food, his next beer, and his army uniforms.

"You want to hear a secret?" she asks to break the stillness. "My husband salutes himself in a mirror. He recites everything he did in the army and salutes the bedroom mirror. He appreciates his accomplishments, which I'm not one of. He likes fried shrimp better than he likes his wife. What can married people do at our age, Buck?"

"Not much," I say. "Will you return when I star in another performance?"

"Ya, I'll come. I look forward to it."

"If I get another gig somewheres, will you come hear me? Maybe they need entertainment at the Moose Lodge or the Elks Club. I'll bring Helen. She's a great lady. You two can meet."

"Ya. Ray'll take me wherever he can have a beer," she says, gently touching her hand to the side of my face. "Too bad we didn't meet when we were young. Too bad we didn't fall in love, Buck."

"Wait," I say. "I hope there's no ketchup on that picnic table. We can sit down. Let's stretch our legs awhile. Come on, I've got a surprise for you, Gusti."

Opening the door to the Pinto, I pull out the accordion case. I lift the beloved instrument from the velvet interior, run my fingers over the buttons and keys, and, thinking of my wife oddly enough, play "Julida Polka" as Gusti leans on the hood of the Pinto.

Her hand on my shoulder as I play, she is smiling, saying "Ya, Buck," as if the beautiful night has anticipated this all along. Our entire lives have anticipated it, I think as I sing, "Julida, Ju-li-da." Never have I sounded better. I could play with anyone, even the great Whoopee John Wilfahrt. Soon I have an audience at the Frostop. I say to Frau Gusti, "Look at that car."

"What car? Where?" Gusti asks.

"The car around there with its lights off."

Her hand on the small of my back, she walks beside me to see who it is.

"Jesus!" she says when she sees the man inside.

"I'm hungry, Gusti!" Ray says.

"I'm hungry, too, Ray. Buck here bought me a fish sandwich to eat."

"How about *my* hungers?" he says, staring at us. "Get in the car, Gusti."

"I don't know if I want to with you drunk. You'll have to drive me, Ray. No more leaving me stranded."

"I'll drive you," he says, puffy chest shrunken a little now. "Who's this with the squeezebox?"

"You know me. Everybody knows me. She told you who I was," I say.

"Did you get hurt when you tangled with the towel dispenser, Ray?" Gusti asks.

"Skinned my knee."

"I suppose you want me to take care of it," she says.

"I've got indigestion, too. I need a Rolaid," he says. "Any place around here to pee?"

Through the passenger side window, I hand him an empty soda pop cup.

Next, opening the door for Gusti, I hold her hand one last time as we listen to Ray relieve himself. I kiss her hand. "You work in the morning anyway, Buck. Let's call it a night. We'll be better off with some sleep," Gusti says.

"Don't go in there with him," I say.

"I have to," she says.

"I guess I can't stand between you if you don't want me to," I say. "But—"

"So long," says Ray, the veteran of a foreign war, as he reaches over to hand me the full cup. "You're no Myron Floren, though you're good enough for the VFW. Look at the moon up there, Gusti."

"Look at it, Buck. Play us a song, something sad while we all look at the moon," Gusti says.

"It's pretty, but no more songs, Frau Gusti. I realize I've got a prior engagement. *Auf Wiedersehen,*" I say to her, thinking, as Ray starts the car, that I will reserve the next polka for my own beautiful wife.

As he backs up, the Big Mouth says, "Empty that cup of piss for me, Mr. Music Man," and sad Gusti is calling, "Good night, Buck Mrozek, and thanks for everything."

Leaves That Shimmer in the Slightest Breeze

IN THE COUNTRY, summer nights come on you in stages. I sat through these stages a hundred times the summer Stanley Dzjduniak came to our farm. As the clock moved from eight-thirty to nine and beyond, darker and darker curtains fell over the hayfields around the house. For ten minutes, I'd watch the well pump house, the wheelbarrow in the yard, or the rutting shed and see no change in the evening light. Then everything grew a little darker. Then for awhile the evening light was unchanged again until another curtain fell and another, 'til finally I could hear the 10:32 rattling its boxcars toward the Fredericka Flour Mill in the East End, and my stepmother or Auntie Ceil would say it was time for a boy to get to bed.

Iron ore trains traveling from open pit mines in northern Minnesota also screeched as they rolled by on the Northern Pacific tracks beyond our fields. The wheat trains going to the mill rode an even grade to the waterfront, but the ore trains started up an earth incline whose grade slowly rose toward a wooden approach structure. Built of criss-crossed beams covered with creosote, the approach led northward for three-quarters of a mile over the roofs of Polish people's houses until it met the main ore dock, one of the three largest in the world. Up on the dock, the trains dumped their load of iron ore into ore pockets, where it was stored until a boat came in. A few years back, the iron ore roared down steel chutes into the holds of the lake boats, but now we didn't hear the ore trains anymore, because the ore dock had been closed down.

The wheat trains still rolled in from western Canada and the Dakotas, however. Their boxcars had CANADIAN WHEAT BOARD or GOUVERNEMENT DU CANADA written on them. The Fredericka mill refined the wheat into flour, which was packed in bags and sent to buyers around the nation. The trains arrived full of wheat and left empty to go for more or left with sacks of flour stacked up to the ceiling. At night, as if looking for someone, the trains' headlamps swept our fields and farm and pried pale fingers into the yard. One minute the house brightened in the train light's glow, and we'd hear the long, loud whistle wail—"Pa-a . . . Pa-a-a-a-a-s-s-s- . . . Comin . . . Pa-a-a-a-s-s-s- . . . Lookin"—and the next minute, the place would lie dark and quiet. Everyone on Polish Road three miles from the East End knew the sound of the train whistles and what the whistles meant to them. For me, the whistles said, "Pa, Pa's comin'. Pa's lookin'!" Even the roses growing on the well pump house took on a strange, beautiful glimmer when the train lights shined on them. They were the same wild roses that clung to the pump house at noon, but in the night you saw them differently.

The summer after my father died, the approach to the abandoned ore dock was torn down. Once the two docks in the Allouez neighborhood were modernized with conveyor belts to carry taconite pellets from inland stockpiles out to the boats, there was no need for the dock in the East End. We heard no ore trains passing; the salvage company had taken steel rails, track spikes, ties, and planking from the approach structure, then left the main dock waiting for the day it might find another purpose. Mr. Dzjduniak had helped tear down the dock. When his work ended, he felt lost and without purpose until the East End neighborhood people who knew him told him to look for work in the country, maybe with the Matuszaks, who were going to sell their farm and move to town. People heard that the Matuszaks needed a barn wrecker. Why not try their place on the Polish Road?

"What can you tell us about a Dzjduniak?" my stepmother Jo and Auntie Ceil asked the salvage company over the phone as Mr. Dzjduniak waited in the kitchen. "He's a worker," the company said. "Harmless enough."

I understood Jo and Ceil's taking precautions, for he was a strong-looking old guy who'd done rough, heavy, dirty work. Still, I wondered what possible harm he could do us when he couldn't breathe right half the time and must've been sixty years old. Though my stepmother and aunt never seemed like it to me before, they were easy marks after all, I guess, and they felt sorry for Mr. "Donuts," which is what the salvage company called him because they couldn't pronounce his name.

"Maybe he has hypertension. That's why his face looks a little red today," Ceil said to us privately. Mr. Dzjduniak's gray hair did make his face appear redder. When I caught him staring at me with blue eyes that saw the trouble you could get into, I'd think, "Stay out of the way. He's someone who has no time for foolishness." The nose bent to one side of his face made him look sad. Sometimes in the yard this worn-out old-timer heaved his shoulders and slumped under a tree, a "quaking aspen," which is called so because its leaves shimmer in the slightest breeze. The aspen was so pretty when the breeze blew and the leaves turned golden in the reflected sunlight. Whether he was tired or not, I learned that when he set to a task, Mr. Donuts could outwork any of us—even me and Willie Czerwinski, the neighbor kid, combined—and Jo and Ceil appreciated his not spitting in the hired man's house, where we put him up.

Right after he arrived they let him know how little I did around our home place. Maybe that's why the barn had to be torn down. Having sold our few cows and pigs, we didn't need an old, leaning barn, a hazard on the property that cost money to insure. Things would've been different if my Pa were alive. In his spare time he'd have kept the farm in order, done something about the barn, and by now would have spread the lime piles that lay on the east part of our land over the earth to sweeten the soil to make hayfields for the day we raised horses. It hurt me watching the changes in the evening light, or talking about Pa, or seeing or doing anything that reminded me of him.

"You say it 'Zhh-doo-nyak,' don't you, Mr. Dzjduniak?" Jo asked that first evening. Railcars being shunted in the yards by the flour mill made a low, faraway bang. When he nodded yes, she went on, "You must be wondering about my husband. He was a switchman on that railroad," Jo said. "Last February we had a heavy snow. They were switching cars in the yards by the flour mill when, oh Lord, he was running through the deep, wet snow on Valentine's Day, and a heart attack took him from us. I cherish him. He was forty-six when he was called to Our Father in heaven. That's how life is. The boy's had his share of misfortune. His mother died when he was seven."

She excused herself then to go in and do the ironing. When I asked could I stay out awhile longer, she said yes, that she would see me and Mr. Dzjduniak in the morning.

With evening dying and leaves shimmering into darkness, we listened to things settle in for the night: a meadow vole scurrying along the barn wall, stopping to listen to Mr. Dzjduniak clear his throat; a robin singing a couple of notes during the twi-

light hour when the dark curtains changed and changed. When
he spoke again, he was a vague outline against the night.

"I lost my own dad when I was a little older than you," he
said. "We didn't have nothing at home, so I had to leave to find
work. I thought I'd like railroading. It'd let me travel the country.
I signed on with a section crew. We went around in a bunk car
that slept ten guys. All day we hid ties, replaced track—all that
bull work for fifty dollars a month. We'd finish a job, and a locomotive would take us somewhere else, mostly through Iowa and
Indiana. Those were bad summers. Blazing hot with no rain. The
corn burnt up. With the dry earth, it was easy for the cinchbugs
to ruin a field. To keep them and rats out, farmers poured oil
around the perimeter. No good. The crops were either eaten up
or rotting. You had to stand by and watch. What could a body
do? I didn't understand any of it. I worked for a railroad. After
work hours I'd go swimming, diving into a river current even if
it meant walking five miles to get there. And all this time those
farmers went under in other ways. Then I switched lines of
work. Hired on at the molasses plant in Dubuque, quit there, got
work on a river barge. But I liked railroading and came back to
it. We'd be off on a siding somewhere in the bunk car when a
passenger train would fly past. You'd see passengers wearing diamond rings in the dining and the club cars. Eventually, that was
gonna be me, I thought, but the last train I rode I hopped in Des
Moines. There were four 'passengers' on it and none of us talked.
It's a hard way to travel, hopping freights."

"My pa would've killed me if I'd ever done that."

"In '49 and '50 I rode regular. I once caught a freight east out
of Chicago. When we stopped to take on water, the fireman
overfilled the tank on purpose and water ran down into the coal
tender, where he'd spotted me hiding. The whole trip it washed
back and forth. Soaked, I dried out and changed directions in

Toledo—as I often would in life. I caught a freight, fell asleep, and woke up on a railroad car ferry on Lake Michigan bound for Milwaukee. It's a tough life."

By the time Jo'd been in the house an hour, the barn wrecker told me a lot more stories. "That late!" he said finally, looking at his railroad watch, then easing out of his chair. "It's enough for tonight."

I waved to him from the back stoop as I went into the house.

With no air stirring the curtains in the room, I lay in bed thinking about him. At eleven, I turned on the radio. "This is the Milwaukee Brewers' Baseball Network," a voice from far away said, then faded out. Across the farm fields, I heard a freight heading in the direction of Chicago and wondered where Mr. Donuts would spend next year.

In the morning he was outside throwing down the shingles and tarpaper I was to rake into piles. I'd work a little then wander off. At noon I'd find him washing up under the pump in the yard. He'd dry his face on the flour sack Jo had hung from the quaking aspen. He'd sip coffee, eat a sandwich, then get back to work. As he climbed up the ladder onto the barn roof, he'd carry the shovel he used for scraping shingles.

By five, down again, he'd need time to rest. I'd call him when Jo told me to. "Mr. Donuts," I'd whisper through the screen door. It took him time to get up from his bed. Once he stretched himself, he was okay, and at supper, which we ate around a table Jo and Ceil set up beneath the aspen tree, he'd tell me stories of other places or of the distinction between a hobo and a bum or of how to jump off a freight or of how to avoid the "bulls," who sometimes chased you in the railroad yards and who carried blackjacks and brass knuckles called dusters. I never tired of hearing his history, such as the lesson he taught me about barn painting. "Done with railroading, I wanted to stay home for awhile," he said. "Then two fellas in an old milkman's delivery truck came past my folks' place. They'd noticed our barn over across the corn and soybean fields from the highway. With my ma's permission, they carried a wood extension ladder out of their truck, propped it against the side of the barn, then way up they started painting a sign they'd pay us to leave up there for advertising purposes. What struck me was that without a guideline, outline, or anything, they could paint a letter, say a *T,* then eyeball in the rest of the sign. It took four hours to finish ours, which, painted in white, said: SUPPORT WISCONSIN'S FARMS.

"I worked in barn painting for a year myself, traveling through Wisconsin and Minnesota. My signs look over the land in Red Wing, Hixson, Alma Center, Sleepy Eye, all over, though I suppose many are gone these days."

"Hey, Mr. Donuts," I said. "We have some paint in our shed."

Jo and Ceil came out just then.

"The paint's hardly good but'll do for a practice if your ma don't mind," he said. "What should he write, Missus? It'll be on a small scale just here close to earth."

"Well," said Ceil, "the official Wisconsin state dance is the polka and we're the second largest ethnic group in Wisconsin, so have him write something Polish, a name or something."

With my finger in the soft earth next to the barn, I wrote two names to guide me, "Casimir Pulaski" and "Frederic Chopin."

Jo and Ceil watched from under the tree as Mr. Dzjduniak, one strong hand holding the brush, carefully, slowly, started painting something else though: a *ZKO.* Then I began. He guided me on an *S.* That was the way to practice—on a barn that was coming down whether you painted the sign right or not.

"I've said it to you before . . . I've done dangerous work. No wheat, coal, or ore in boxcars is worth the effort. This has all got a message, son," he told me. "People are worth risking something for, but not railroads. Here, go an eighth-inch higher on that *U*," he said. I did, painting as he talked.

"I never cared, as a youth, for things that really mattered," he was saying, "not for honesty or for honest people. Not being one myself, I wanted only to get rich. But I should have cared about them. After trying barn painting, I got into working salvage where you clean out derailed or damaged boxcars. Had myself quite an operation. If I met other boys lookin' for the derailment, I'd send 'em off down the wrong road so that I got to the derailment first to make sure I got hired. The railroad needed you to clean out cars so they could get them back on track and clear the line. Trouble was, when too many men showed up, there wasn't enough work to go around. When that happened and I was broke and hungry, I had to make a few dollars any way I could, honest or dishonest.

"There's no way to justify stealing another's property or a company's goods and products, then selling them. I lost heart for that kind of activity. I wanted the honesty of a good man's life, had observed others defy natural impulses to lie, steal, and cheat when well they might have done so. If these hobos you saw riding the rails could fight down their bad impulses, I could too, I figured. After that, whenever guys came by and asked 'Where's the wreck we heard about?' I'd let them follow me to it. And after that whenever I was penniless and saw something I might filch and sell for a few bucks, I walked right past and out of temptation."

Why was he telling *me*? I wondered. Maybe I didn't work around the place much, but I'd been straight with Jo and Ceil. He seemed to be dreaming as he watched me paint letters on the barn. I liked seeing him resting from the hard work of tearing down the barn, which he always stopped by four or five in the afternoon. A couple of days later, he was down to the rafters and resting more often. With me sitting beside him, he'd tell how all those years he should've stayed on the farm instead of roaming around. But now in late middle age he'd found a place he'd like to remain awhile if Jo didn't begrudge him.

By then I'd finished the name "Tadeusz Kościuszko," which is the Polish spelling, and was painting words beneath it. By a vase of dried flowers Jo kept on Pa's old desk was a postcard with dues information on it from the Polish Club in town. The Kosciuszko Lodge, it's called. Pa kept the card ever since he'd first joined the club. Along with a portrait of Thaddeus Kosciuszko, the card told about that great historical figure who

> served with George Washington and fortified West Point, commanded a corps against the Russians in 1792, and in Poland led the Insurrection against them in 1794. His edicts enfranchised all peasants who fought for Poland. He freed the black slaves given to him by the United States Congress and sold all his lands in America to pay for the freedom of other slaves.

Now I was painting under the great name "Kościuszko" these words: AMERICAN REVOLUTIONARY HERO. My brush still wet, I worked on the *ARY* part as Mr. Dzjduniak went on with his stories. It was like a toast, I thought. I *was* making a toast. To a Grand Old Gent. To Mr. Stanley Dzjduniak and to Mr. Tadeusz Kościuszko. Especially to the fellow who traveled all around on trains . . . who taught me lessons about adventures and how to find them . . . and who'd helped me, Jo, and Ceil around here.

As I stacked shingles or painted signs advertising Polish history, he tore down the barn. Though I was afraid of heights and couldn't climb the ladder with him, me and the old guy were still a couple of brave and heroic barn wreckers in spirit.

Then August. I watched as he drew closer to us. From up near peak and rafter, he'd worked downward to the foundation, which I thought was solid like him. Unfortunately, *I* hadn't learned his moral lessons and teaching very well—at least I hadn't during one afternoon that summer. Watching him, hearing his stories, which he'd yell down to me—such things made me want to do something brave as well. When only a few boards and the stone foundation were left of the barn, and when the raspberries were ripe and the corn ripening, Willie Czerwinski dared me to follow him on an adventure. He was a year older than me, and I didn't like him, but he was the only kid my age to hang around with. Sometimes one of his teeth poked out between his lips. Patches of brown hair stuck up from his head like radio antennas. When his father cut the patches, Willie's head looked like it had bruises on it. He cursed a lot. He told me to meet him by the tracks. We hid in a grove of birches. When the train came by, barely crawling, it was pulling forty empties. When it speeded up, Willie ran beside a boxcar, climbed in, then lifted me up and in. They left a lot of wheat in the empties, and he started sweeping it like crazy.

He'd brought burlap bags to brush the wheat into. Inside, the boxcar was high-ceilinged and drafty, its walls lined with smooth boards. The boxcar pitched from side to side. I never knew railroad cars echoed your family's name. This one creaked and swayed and called out to me.

With my cap I swept wheat into a bag. The old-fashioned cap with a snap brim had belonged to my father. The band on the inside of it soon got wheat in it. Then I lost my balance. I wished I was on top of the barn—anywhere but here. But that was part of the past. Hardly any barn was left. "Sweep faster," said Willie. The tooth poking out of his mouth made him look like he was angry at me and his life.

Willie'd sell the wheat or feed his pa's chickens. I couldn't find my legs as the train went faster. We had three sacks and part of a fourth when he jumped out. I held to the inside of the rolling boxcar. Through the door, I saw track ballast and weeds and heard him yelling, "Jump, stupid Polack!" But I couldn't. The boxcar's rocking made it hard to keep my balance. By now the train seemed like it was going ninety miles an hour when I heard the whistle—Pa-a-a-a- . . . Pa-a-s-s-s- . . . Comin . . . Pa! World rushing past, I got sick. What'd become of Jo and Ceil? Hanging onto the cap, I leapt out as far as I could into the afternoon.

Willie stood over me laughing. When he saw my face, he got serious. My hands hurt. I'd gouged them on clinkers. Part of a clinker was still in one hand. "C'mon, you gotta get home," he said. I had blood in my eyes. My head throbbed. Willie couldn't look at me. "What you gonna do?" he asked. "You got a cut on your forehead." He told me to pull the cap down over it as we ran. I was dizzy. I could make it home, I said. I was all right.

When Willie left, I ran past the lime piles through the field holding my cap against the bleeding. I felt my leg burning inside the overalls. When I thought of the train, the smoke, the banging, I got sick and had to stop running. I felt closer to the barn wrecker, though. We had something in common. We'd done dangerous things. I didn't know if it was worth it doing this. Still, if you wanted to be a man of experience, you had to pull daring exploits.

Ceil fainted when I got home. Jo pulled me close, then dragged me to the pump. The barn wrecker drew cold water as Jo dabbed the cut.

"I fell," I told her. "I cut my head on the concrete in front of the East End Coast-to-Coast store."

Before I could finish, she was asking why nobody fixed the streets and sidewalks in town. She kept washing my forehead.

"It'll need stitches," said the barn wrecker. "We'll get you to the doc."

I wondered whether he admired how I fought the pain or whether he'd ever seen such a bad cut. Then I made a mistake. When I put my cap back on, some wheat fell out. I looked at Jo. Rinsing the rag, she hadn't seen the wheat. But the barn wrecker did. Leaning against the tree with the shimmering leaves, Mr. Dzjduniak saw what fell out of Pa's cap.

"Where'd you say you took the tumble, son?"

Something in his voice made Jo turn. Her eyes followed where he pointed his finger. When she looked at the wheat, I saw her face change.

"Where?" she asked doubtfully.

"The Coast-to-Coast."

"What's wheat doing in the cap?" she asked.

"What wheat?" I said, but it was no use lying to them. "Ah, it's nothing," I said. But it *was* something, what Mr. Dzjduniak did to me. I was angry and surprised by his telling on me. I didn't care how he felt anymore, just about Jo. I looked at the wild roses on the barn and pump house, the prickly stems along the trellis. I looked at the wheat fallen from the cap. I could see the barn wrecker had been working. The barn was down, and I'd hardly helped. He'd turned on me. Why? I wondered. I was crying then—more because I'd lied and he'd told on me than because of any cut on the forehead. I cried, too, because of how we'd sold the few hogs we had and had torn down the barn. Jo, me, and Ceil would be alone soon, the summer gone. It wasn't what happened to my forehead or hand that made me cry, or that I had no courage for barn wrecking, sweeping wheat, or anything like that. It was everything—the sight of the aspen trees, the Kościuszko sign, the wild roses on the pump house wall. I'd never felt as bad—for Jo, Mr. Donuts, Ceil, myself. I didn't know what got into me to lie nor how I'd see it right. On top of it, I'd sullied Pa's name, and this was something I'd have to live with.

Ashamed, I stayed in my room the next couple of evenings. I thought about our good name and honor. My father's booklet of Polish Club rules said that "the President and all members should conduct themselves as gentlemen in public and private." If I wanted to join the club someday, I'd have to be a little better in my life. I believed Pa would be happy if I joined. Pa would be pleased if I worked more around here, too, for Jo and Ceil had enough to do. Listening to train whistles late one night, I decided I'd have to make some changes.

First thing the next morning I found among the stacks of weathered barn boards the one I'd painted the name "Kościuszko" on. Somebody'd put the board on top of one of the piles. I brought it into the house. Then I asked Mr. Donuts and everyone what I could do to help out.

"Cut the lawn," Jo said.

"Burn the trash in the barrel," Ceil said.

"There's laundry to hang out," Jo said.

Though they were mainly teasing me, I did as they said while Mr. Donuts watched. I also swept the sidewalk, did supper dishes, and helped him fix the window screens in the hired man's house.

By summer's end, by the time the school buses started rolling down the farm roads to bring us all back again, something had changed in my life. The barn I'd been so afraid of climbing was gone, and I was a little older.

I remember the barn wrecker telling me after I'd worked hard for two weeks, "I'll be leaving your aunt and stepma soon, but I want you to know something, son. You became a true workman toward the end here. You became a man, because I know how bad you felt the day you let Jo and Ceil down, and I know what you've done to fix that. I'm proud of how it's turned out these past few weeks."

He shook my hand, gave me a hug.

I believed him when he complimented me about taking responsibility, and I still do today, though we never again heard from him. I believed him all through junior high and high school, because he was a sign painter, barn wrecker, salvage man, and hobo all rolled into one, and he never lied, not Mr. Donuts, Mr. Dzjduniak, with his wrecking tools and stories of the road.

The Moon of the Grass Fires

ABOVE THE FLOUR MILL it appeared as though the body of Jesus Christ hung in the fine waves of wheat dust. People would say it was an optical illusion created by the dust, but why not this reflection of Christ when twenty-four hours a day the mill refined wheat into the flour Catholic bakers use? From around the country, laity and nuns in the bakers' trade wrote letters saying what exceptional Eucharistic flour it was. Of course, St. Adalbert's Church used communion wafers made from wheat milled at the Fredericka, so there was also a customer base right in Joe Lesczyk's hometown.

Now retired, Joe Lesczyk (his grandfather Lesczynski had shortened the name when he came to America) could relax without worrying about the mill. For eight hours five days a week for forty years, he'd oiled motors, laid conduit, packed flour—done a dozen dusty chores at the mill. Seeing himself in the mirror, he shook his head sadly, thinking how he looked like an old man who'd slept in a perpetual blizzard all his life, which really isn't far from truth, given northern Wisconsin's climate. However, it wasn't ice or snow but semolina dust come to the fine map of Joe Lesczyk's face, much as the autumn frost settles in ravines and swamps and on the gardens and fields of East End. How many years since he was young? Joe Lesczyk wondered.

A week after his retirement the year before, an odd thing had happened to him. He'd come into possession of a church confessional, a plain, wooden, rectangular structure that stood five feet high, eight or nine feet long, perhaps four across. He got it when one of the Slovaks of the parish, the successful corner grocery store owner, Mrs. Bendis, contributed money for a new confessional. This being Father Nowak's *Jubileusz kapłanstwa*, his Silver Jubilee Anniversary, what better gift than a more stylish confessional for the priest Nowak? Because Joe Lesczyk couldn't stand seeing the old one hauled off to an industrial waste landfill, where the crucifix would poke out from demolition debris, he asked the parish council if he could have the confessional.

Sin is not light, of course. A confessional can weigh six hundred pounds or more. How difficult it was for the boys he hired to lift it into the rusty bed of a pickup truck. On the way down East Fourth Street to Joe Lesczyk's two-car garage, the purple confessional curtains danced gaily in the breeze. Then at the house, the boys slid the confessional out an inch at a time so they could get hold of it and carry it into the garage, where they set it down in a corner.

Now that the confessional was "decommissioned" and he was alone with it, Joe Lesczyk, more contemplative in retirement, thought how for ninety years sinners—shadowy, immobile, pensive—had knelt on these very kneelers waiting for one priest or another to slide open the wooden door to the screen separating penitent from confessor. Saturday after Saturday a priest had sat in the lonely box.

Through almost his entire life, Joe Lesczyk had also knelt in this confessional, on one side of which a placard read: CONFESSIONS IN POLISH HEARD HERE. Envy, covetousness, lewd thoughts, taking God's name in vain—so often he'd burdened the old priest Father Marciniak and later his replacement, Father Nowak, with his sins. What could they have thought? True, a cloth screen separated them from him and, true, the light in the confessional booth was dim, but the priests still knew which parishioner was here to whisper of spiritual failure. Now that he was proud owner of a confessional, it seemed to him as if he could reclaim his sins from it.

"Mister, they shoulda never painted this thing," a furniture stripper, a non-Catholic, told him a few days later. "Looks like they had good paint back then. Makes it hard to get it off when the paint's so good." At first the refinisher thought it was a kids' playhouse. He wanted $750 to haul the confessional out of Joe's garage to his shop, there to suspend it in a vat of paint remover for as long as it took to strip off the paint. "It'll be the first and last I'll ever do," he said. "A lot of work. I suppose you Catholics would say there's sin in the walls, even in the nails."

The real sin was how much the refinisher would charge, Joe Lesczyk thought. That's when he decided to hire a couple of the neighborhood boys, the movers, to strip the whole thing down, then put on a good coat of lacquer to enhance the beautiful wood he imagined lay beneath. They could brush on paint remover, scrape off the layers of enamel with a putty knife, and so could he when he felt up to it. Working a few days a week, in six months they'd have a good conversation piece. It'd be a retirement project. It would be cheaper this way, too: the economical, hands-on way of cleaning off the yellowing past of sinfulness that had formed a patina on the walls. If the garage got too cluttered, maybe in time he would donate the fresh, clean confessional to the historical society.

When he'd taken down the two curtains plus the one that'd hidden the priest in the center part, the phone rang. He'd left the living room window and the front door open so he could hear the phone.

"I'm fine," he said when his wife asked. She was in Florida, visiting their daughter Meg. "Everything okay in St. Petersburg?"

"We're doing great. You okay, Joe?"

"I'm okay. Meg okay?"

"We're fine," said Barbara.

"Guess what? I'm working on our retirement project."

"What?"

"You remember. From St. Adalbert's. I asked a furniture stripper to quote me a price."

"I'm starting to worry about you. Are you feeling okay?" said his wife.

"I feel great. The thing is the confessional," he said. "We can confess to each other. I'm going to try some paint remover myself on it in a minute."

"Will you call me later? Please tell me you're all right."

"Sure I'll call," he said. "And I couldn't be happier. Hey, I'm retired. If there's something you want to confess, let me know, Barbara."

"This comes as a surprise. I'll call you when the news sinks in. What does anyone need a confessional for?"

"To find out about ourselves and why we sin," he said.

"Don't learn too much," she said. "Wait 'til I get back."

• • •

After the first hour of stripping paint, he realized the job was bigger than he thought. The confessional seemed larger without curtains. It had been built big to accommodate the gruff workers with mortal sins needing confession and absolution—railroad car knockers, ore punchers, sailors off the lake boats, millhands guilty of terrible deeds. All those years of sinning. He worked for another hour with cloth and scraper, then, cautioning himself to slow down, reminding himself he was retired, he sat awhile in the priest's side of the confessional. He recalled some of the parishioners who'd knelt to confess: Mrs. Pilsudski, Michael Zimski, the Milszewski boy with a Purple Heart, Louie Stefanko. He recalled how rarely Mr. Zielinski observed the Fourth Commandment, how it was whispered that Mr. Dzelak was remiss in areas of life covered by the Fifth Commandment, how Mr. Marsolek, Mr. Novazinski, and Mrs. Petruska, the school teacher, were remiss in the Sixth Commandment. As though someone were in the garage to hear him, he called out his parents' names as among the sinners. What a silly thing, to sit alone in retirement and say names aloud to yourself. He repeated relatives' names, repeated his own and his wife's names, but when he said "Mother" again, as though asking her something he'd wondered about, he broke the stillness in such a way that he felt it would be better to leave the confessor's center part to kneel in one of the penitent's boxes. "Bless me, Father, for I have sinned . . . ," he said and began, as a kind of Examination of Conscience, to retell the passions of his and his mother's lives.

He remembered her in the kitchen years before saying, "Do it for me, Joseph." Over half a century earlier, he'd knelt in the back pew of St. Adalbert's Church and wondered, "Have I neglected my parents in their necessity?"

"Dad says no. I'm not supposed to go to the drugstore for you. He says the stuff makes you sick and crazy."

"You can do it for me," she implored. He was nine, ten perhaps. Life had passed so quickly since then. Now he himself was old.

"For me, Joe. Run an errand for your mom. Sure, you won't mind doing that. You're a good boy."

It was a fine afternoon this time she'd wanted her Asthmador

Powder. He was on his way to play football with the neighbor boys. "Just take your bike and run an errand to the drugstore for me," she said.

"No, I can't, Mother."

Why she hadn't pulled on a sweater and walked to the store herself, he couldn't understand. "Please, Joe, go after it for me?" she asked again. "Then deliver this note to Mr. Mrozek."

How blue the sky was back then but for that slight smoke haze in the distance. Every autumn, people set fire to their vacant lots and fields and burned their piles of leaves.

Now, not so many years later, needing to leave the confessional, he decided to rake leaves beneath the apple tree for an hour. Over the yards and fields, daydreams hovered in the smoke. He remembered his mother in the kitchen, wearing her maroon bathrobe with its sagging pockets, her hair uncombed. Though not intending to startle her son, to steady herself, she grabbed his shirtsleeves. He kept telling her he didn't want to go to the store for her or to deliver any messages to the neighbor, an accordion player whose house lay across and down a dusty alley. "I won't go over to Buck Mrozek's," Joe Lesczyk said to his mother. "No more requests for Buck Mrozek." He said it now as he picked an apple from the tree.

During the warmer months, you could hear Buck Mrozek practicing his music. He left the kitchen window open or practiced the accordion right out in his backyard. Everyone loved him, especially Joe Lescyzk's mother. During an evening, you never heard the same song twice, and, with his expensive accordion and the finest Frankie Yankovic sheet music collection in northern Wisconsin, Buck took requests. Even Joe himself liked to hear Buck play. Seeing the neighbor boy admiring him, Buck would smile, break into "She's Too Fat Polka" in honor of one of the Polish ladies passing down the alley, and shout over the music

" Hoo-yaa-yaa." A "hoo-hoo-hoo" or "yoo-hoo-hoo" could be heard from neighboring houses.

Now years later with the moon rising over the smoke, the retired millhand expected the music but instead heard the phone ring.

"Dad, is that you?" the voice said. "Sorry we haven't talked. I've been busy," Meg said.

"I was outside," he said.

"How's retirement?"

"Fine. I was outside being retired. Guess what? I'm having an apple."

"Wish I could join you. Aren't they good?"

"How's your ma?"

"Fine. We're watching the baby."

"Did I tell you I'm having an apple from your grandfather's tree?"

"Enjoy it. You deserve it."

"The moon's out early. The air smells like fire. It's people burning their leaves. It's the best time of year. Remember autumn evenings in Superior?"

"You deserve autumn," Meg said. "You worked hard all your life to get there. Look at how our time's gone. I've gotta go. I've gotta check on the baby."

She hung up.

"Meg?" he said, noticing as he sat with the receiver in his hand that the moon was following him into the room.

Its light stayed with him until ten-thirty, until midnight. When he arose at two-thirty and went downstairs, there it was: the moon. Opening the living-room drapes, he watched the apple tree throw its moonlit shadows over the strange, yellow-silver night.

Years ago he'd stood in the kitchen, his mother balancing

herself against the table. On a plate she'd pour a little pile of the green powder she'd light with a stick match. She leaned forward to inhale the gray-green smoke. Stumbling sideways, she'd say, "Deliver the note. I'm out. Go to the store for your mother, Joey."

He'd thrown on his jacket . . . was standing in the back shed that led into the kitchen. His father was at work.

"He doesn't want me to, Dad doesn't," he'd said.

It was who might have seen her, he thought, that's why his mother, a married woman, a Catholic, wouldn't carry a note with a polka request down the alley or get the can of Asthmador Powder for her breathing. Stumbling like that, she couldn't walk to the drugstore. None of it made sense back then when his father asked the druggist not to sell her the medication. "Don't go for her if she asks you to, Joe, and I'm at work," his dad said.

"Oh, please, Joey," she'd say. "I'm gonna fall down on this floor and get very sick."

"I can't help you," he'd tell her. "It's a sin for me to run your errands."

"Hug me," she'd say and give him seventy-five cents for her Asthmador Powder.

Later when he sat across from her at the kitchen table, thick smoke rose about her face and she was calm. "Did you go across the alley for me, too? Did you tell Buck to play 'The East End Polka'?"

"I told him."

"What did he say?"

"He said, 'Yoo-hoo-hoo.'"

"Not 'hoo-hoo-hoo'? Are you sure you're not mixed up?"

"No. You're the one that's mixed up," Joe said.

"Don't speak like that to your mother. Haven't you learned anything from your catechism? What does it say about respect for our parents, about not abandoning our mothers in their necessity?"

His mother started getting crazy again, talking faster. "Examine your conscience. Study the *Baltimore Catechism*. Don't fail me in life. Buck's famous for 'The East End Polka.' He could've toured with Whoopee John Wilfahrt or played with Dick Contino's band. Buck's a good, decent neighbor. What do you know about polka? You come here. Ma wants you to dance with her."

Clapping her hands, she got up a polka beat. "You sing along, Joey. Buck wrote this song:

> She lives in East End,
> I live in Nord' End.
> I work the shipyard,
> She works the bakery.
> When we're in East End—

Come on, Joey!"

"'We dance the polka,'" he sang the next line and the next as she swayed so hard he felt sick to his stomach watching her.

When she polkaed nearer to him, he hid from her on the back porch. That day for the first time he noticed that his mother's dress, too tight about the stomach, had spots on the sleeves and that her arms sagged with flesh. Her hair had started to gray. He watched her dance until she slumped down in a chair, laid her head on the table, and cried. She'd had a catharsis, a kind of polka catharsis.

"'We dance the polka. Oh, aren't we happy?'" he sang softly to her from the porch after five minutes.

"No, we aren't happy unless you run her errands for your mother, Joey, just across the alley with requests. You've gotta go fast before Dad gets home."

"I won't fail you in your necessity," Joe said.

. . .

Stella Lesczyk's breathing never improved. She'd used the smoking powder a long time before a new doctor made her stop. "There's belladonna in it," the doctor told his father. Sometimes Joe couldn't remember the name—belladonna—but he remembered how his father was furious with his wife when he came home the day she was dancing. Joe remembered her begging her husband not to be angry, remembered her saying she couldn't help it if she was addicted. She'd make his favorite noodle dish if he wouldn't be angry. "It's the asthma powder that gets her," Mr. Lesczyk was telling his son. "It has nothing to do with polka. She shouldn't give polka a bad name."

Years later—Mr. Lesczyk having preceded her in death—she lay in a hospital, heart enlarged from the asthma. Face flushed from coughing, she wanted Joe to hold her hand. Instead, he wiped her mouth with a napkin, threw the napkin in the wastebasket, then stepped out. When he did, her coughing stopped. In the hospital waiting room, a now ancient Buck Mrozek sat with his accordion. He showed Joe a new arrangement of an old standard. It was as if Buck was seeking the right combination of words and polka music to keep Mrs. Lesczyk alive. She was his biggest fan; he was the undisputed polka king of East End. "Please get better, Ma," Joe, her son, was pleading, but that day she died, and he, Joe Lesczyk of Fredericka Flour, had to tell Buck to put away the accordion. Some years later, the king himself, Buck Mrozek, died, leaving his music to his son.

Now with the moon over the harvest fields, Joe Lesczyk thought of calling his wife in Florida, but when he looked at the clock, it was three in the morning.

Despite his joy, each day brought sadness, for he was understanding the mystery and pain of life. When the breezes blew, the maple tree in the yard shimmered in sunlight—a delicate time in his retirement. When he looked at the confessional, he noticed how the wood, though covered with paint long ago, was still smooth to the touch. The old people were dead, but here he stayed thinking of them, their lives growing into the one big mystery that included the image of Christ reflected in dust over the mill.

Not much was said about Stella Lesczyk's addiction. She'd stopped using the smoking powder, and no one talked about it, and to her son it was a memory. Dreams, myster . . . , *memories;* they get mixed up.

"Bless me, Father, for I have sinned," he said—the opening words of the Form of Confession. Instead of kneeling in the confessional, he decided to look in an old dresser in the garage for the broken dinner plate she had used for a smoking dish. He wished to have it, the burnt part, to smell the thick, bitter dreams of childhood. "I'm home," he was saying out loud. No one was there to hear. "I'll be back in the house in a moment. Do you want anything? I'm practicing the Form of Confession out here in the garage. 'Bless me, Father, for I have sinned.' It's the confessional all of you knelt in."

He spoke aloud to his parents, to his aunts and uncles. He told them he had more time to think of them now. He wondered if they could hear him. "I'm in the garage," he told their ghosts again. "I never wanted to disappoint any of you," he said as if, so long after she died, his mother could hear him. Christ in the mystery of confession, in the mystery of the Eucharist, knew what was happening to Joseph Lesczyk in his retirement.

"Please, Joe-Sweetie. Take a minute to go to the drugstore for me on your bike."

"No," said Joe Lesczyk, who thought he heard a polka. "No," he said again now in retirement.

• • •

Memory was his retirement problem—not health concerns, not financial worries. Remembering was the problem. He'd rake leaves, then dwell on autumn and winter themes. As he waited for the moon, he knew nobody in his family ever died in summer. They died when it was bitter cold and cemetery workers had to plow the snow, then thaw a section of ground with torches so they could dig in it. His mother died on All Souls' Day, his father in an earlier year eight days before Christmas. Both times Joe Lesczyk, Fredericka employee, came to confession. To receive the Holy Eucharist, whose wheat he milled, he had to be pure of heart. In winter were deaths and disappointments. During the bitter season a man counts on them. But not in summer. No summer disappointments. He'd made it to retirement.

Now fall had come and with it the moon of the grass fires. He'd often wondered how long to defer payment on the past. Then this evening, the moon, bigger than any this autumn, rose right down at the end of the street, where it insisted on staying. He'd been raking leaves, listening to music drift over the air (the high school band preparing for homecoming, he thought) when, just as he was about to forgive his mother for requesting "The East End Polka" so often all those years, the yellow-eyed moon took his breath away.

It was so aged and huge, that harvest moon intruding at the end of Fourth Street, that he started walking toward it as if it had something special to tell him. The neighbors wondered why he was heading away from the church and the flour mill, where they'd seen him coming and going all his life. Now they saw him head in this new direction, because a light breeze that carries the flour dust with it had come up; he wasn't walking against it but with the breeze. If you are a believer, you'd say, perhaps only a little fancifully, that he was walking in the direction of the holy garments of Jesus Christ, enjoying the protection of His gentle shimmering robes. Almost imperceptibly at first, the amber dust from wheat that would eventually be made into Christ's Body in the Eucharist settled onto the former millhand.

"Hello, Joe Lesczyk," people called as they passed. "How's retirement?"

"Fine," he answered. Then, with his eyes on the moon, he said, "Look how old the moon grows. What mysteries! It shined on Jesus in the garden, on Jesus on the cross. Lord, forgive us all."

A group of boys started following him on bikes the way Joe Lesczyk, on his own bicycle as a youth, would have followed someone like him on an autumn evening. They were good children. Trained by the nuns at St. Adalbert's, they knew both their Form of Confession and their Prayers for the Adoration of the Eucharist. Eventually some of their parents joined them.

"You're full of dust, Mr. Lesczyk," they called to him.

When he stopped and made the sign of the cross on his forehead he said, "Yes, I finally see that."

At the abandoned ore dock, he stopped again with his flock. From there you can plainly observe what the moon of the grass fires illuminates—a valley, a railroad trestle, a Left-Handed River. Joe Lesczyk saw his entire life, remembered his hard-working father, remembered the pain his mother'd caused them.

Now a few curious boys rode closer to him so they could touch his sleeve to watch dust rise. "You're *really* full of dust now, Mr. Lesczyk," they said. In the soft breeze, the wheat dust fell lightly on all of them, the amber dust of the Lamb of God.

"May the Body of Our Lord, Jesus Christ, keep our souls," he said.

Hearing the retired millhand, the boys began to notice the dust on themselves; but, because they were young and hadn't seen much of life's sorrows, at first they made no connection between themselves, Joe Lesczyk, and the Body of Our Savior on this beautiful autumn evening.

It Had To Be You

SO WHO CARES if I'm a broken-down biddy with spider veins on her legs? Once I slip on my tap shoes, there's no stopping me. I give 'em a Tampa or two, go into an Indian Two-Step. Here's the rhythm of your basic Tampa: scuff, hop, toe, heel, toe-step, brush-step, ball-change. Say them like they're separate words. Say them fast, "brush-step, ball-change," and you get that distinctive Tampa beat. Oh, I can tap dance! Watch me Shim-Sham! Watch me Wind the Clock!

"So you Wind the Clock, Ethel," my husband, Eddie, says. "Now work on your Tea-for-Two a little."

"I *am* already. Patience," I tell him.

"We haven't practiced, so come on," he says. "We've got another show coming up."

Years of following lousy comedians, plate spinners, and unicyclists have taken their toll on us. To humor Eddie, I give him a Tea-for-Two, which is three brush-steps, brush toe-steps in a circle. Here's another step: "It had to be you (scuff, hop, toe, heel . . . back-step, brush-step, ball-change). It had to be you" (scuff, hop, toe, heel . . .).

Eddie's a Jew. I'm a Polish Catholic lady. "Work on your

Back Irish and trust me," he said when we first performed at the
Savoy on Tower Avenue in Superior, Wisconsin, in '43. Joe
Howard, Eddie Cantor, Georgie Jessel, Walter Winchell, Flo
Cushman . . . "the Diamond Tooth Girl"—they all worked the
Savoy and went on to bigger or smaller things.

That we never became stars is disappointing. Audiences
laughed at us. I never knew why. Everywhere in the country we
were last on the bill. Clowns, magicians, comedians, animal acts
preceded us. In Blooming Prairie, Minnesota, we were once
upstaged by a flea circus. "*Oy vey ist mir,*" Eddie said. In August
'47, in Superior, Wisconsin, again—this time in a "gigantic two-
hour stage show" outdoors at the Superior Blues ballpark—we
followed (1) Rudy Vallee and his orchestra; (2) Lalo and Musette,
"Adagio Act"; (3) Clark and Durant, comedians; (4) the Ayers
Sisters, baton twirlers; (5) "Golden, the Magician"; (6) Doris
King, "Thrilling Voice of Stage and Screen"; and (7) Tinkers, the
Trained Seal. Ten o'clock at night, everybody including Eddie's
relatives gone home, fog rolling in off Lake Superior, and out we
come to play to a deserted ballpark. Halfway through the third
number, which we dance without music, the stadium lights go
off. We're standing in center field, foghorns blowing, ore trains
rattling past behind the scoreboard. Troupers that we are, we
dance 'til our programme's over and the stadium crew tells us to
get out.

That was it for Eddie. No more show biz ever! "*Oy vey,*" he
said again. We took the passenger train out in the morning. Lalo
and Musette were aboard. They were tired of the business, too.
Lalo had a flask. We sat in the smoking car drinking, talking
about the ugly town we were leaving, Eddie's hometown, where
there's that settlement of Jews down on Connors' Point. Lalo said
Superior was uglier than Oakland. Musette said, "No, it isn't,
Lalo."

The next week my husband, Eddie, considered a career in sales. "What does everybody need these days? What's indispensable to the modern office?" he asked. (We were in Joliet. You could see the penitentiary from the hotel window.) For the next two weeks, he sold *carbon paper*! He'd buy a box at Kresge's, then go office to office charging his marked-up price. Secretaries and office managers thought the Carbon Paper Man was a hoot. He'd stand in the middle of their office and bow to them, pretending he was on stage at the Gaiety in D.C. What a scene with all these secretaries laughing at him, him doing a Back Irish out the door and telling me in the alley, "Sorry, Ethel, no sale."

"We gotta get back into show business, Eddie," I said.

When we started up tap dancing again, I thought this time we'd make it: We played Rochester, New York, in '49 . . . left 'em crying for more at the Auto Show in Detroit in '50 . . . Milwaukee, St. Paul, St. Louis, Memphis, Shreveport, Pascagoula, Mobile. After a two-week gig in New Orleans, we were headed north where the *Kansas City Star* newspaper ad read:

> See the Special 3-Unit Full-Length, Big-Time Burlesque Show. Featuring Sunra, Sun-Bathed Nature Girl . . . Texas Rae, Sweetheart of Texas . . . Rickey Rich, New Orleans Fashion Plate Woman Impersonator.
> Plus
> 8 ace funsters, 20 sassy lassies, 8 beautiful dancers . . . You'll laugh a lot . . . you may blush a little . . . but you won't be bored. We dare not tell you more.
> Plus
> Eddie and Ethel, Dancing Couple.

Did we ever get a mention in *Variety*? No. Still, I was with him all the way.

Our exclusive engagement in K.C. was extended a month.

We danced to "Tico Tico" . . . "Chiri Biri Bin." In one production number, I was a naive traveler in a country of hot-blooded men. Stage dark, a yellow spot would pick me up stage right. I wore a rose-colored dress, chiffon so it would flow better, and matching shoes. Then Eddie would enter stage left—sleek, handsome Eddie, his black shirt open to the waist, his rose-colored sash knotted at the hip, his black pants and shoes. My coyness, Eddie's worldliness, we brought down the house, I tell you, when we did that final brush-step, ball-change. We'd eat a quick meal at a diner on Prospect, then hurry to the theater for evening shows. It was a relief to get out of the simmering heat and back into the "Refrigeration Cooled" Princess Theater.

"Let's stay in the theater tonight," Eddie would say after the last show. "Let's not both of us trudge back to our hotel. It's so hot you'll bake. I'll run over, check on things, grab a bite to bring you back—those K.C. ribs you like. I can take the heat better."

"Sure, Ed. Ribs'll be great. Bring me a Bromo-Seltzer."

If I wasn't bushed and my dogs weren't aching, I'd go out for a half-hour to Union Station or walk toward the Paseo, trying to get a breeze off the Missouri. After two weeks of walking the streets alone, I realized I was fooling myself. Night after night, Eddie tells me to stay put on the divan in the smokers' loge of a Kansas City theater while he runs off somewhere in his black shirt and rose sash, his stage makeup on . . . night after night a husband who tells me he can take the heat when he really hates and despises heat and gets crabby in it. Still in love with him, I tried to convince myself nothing was wrong after seven years of happy marriage.

When the marquee lights went off, when the doors were locked and only the exit lights burned inside the theater, I'd walk onstage. I could never go it alone. I realized all over again that

Eddie and Ethel were made for each other. The Dorics, Bijous, and Lyrics we played were grand with plush carpeting, muraled lobbies, marble stairways to balconies and side boxes. When Eddie left me alone, I got to know the Princess as well as any theater. I'd wander the aisles, circle the orchestra pit, rest in the loge upstairs. When was Eddie Cohen returning to get me? Did I have to sleep alone on a couch? Couldn't we make whoopee?

Our hotel room, where I realized he didn't want me to come, was on Eighteenth Street. If the evening wasn't too hot, he'd make other excuses to get away from me: He needed time alone, he didn't want to be disturbed, he was practicing a new step, he didn't want to bother anyone in the theater. Bother who? I was the only one staring out the dark ticket window at three in the morning. Maybe he *was* telling the truth and really did need to be alone to practice, but I had my doubts.

When I found the courage to go to the hotel to investigate, just as I suspected I could hear him talking to someone. It sounded like they were telling jokes. I heard Eddie saying, "So these two drunks are stumbling down the Kansas City and Southern railroad tracks when one says, 'Oh, my achin' head.'" Then I heard another voice deliver the punch line: "Head nothing. These stairs are killing me!" An odd, shrill voice laughed once it told the joke about the drunks.

When I knocked at my own hotel room door, that same voice said, "Don't open it, Eddie. Don't open that door!" The hall stunk of cabbage.

"Who've you got inside?" I asked Eddie through the door.

"Don't be dumb. Is that you, Ethel?" he asked. "I'm here alone."

"Who's in there? You can't fool me."

"Don't be dumb," the strange voice said. Then it began singing, "It had to be you."

"Open the door. I've got my tap shoes. I'm gonna do a Shim-Sham in the hallway and wake everyone in the hotel, Eddie."

Now Eddie's and the stranger's voices were singing, "It had to be you . . . wonderful you. . . ."

"Is it Sunra, Sun-Bathed Nature Girl, in there with you?" I asked.

"What're you talking about? Does he sound like a woman? I've gotta practice that voice more."

When I opened the door, Eddie sat on the edge of the bed, his face and shirt wet with sweat. The dummy sat on his lap in that dreary room.

"Say hi to the lady, Vincento," Eddie said.

"Hi, lady," said Vincento. Eddie's lips didn't move.

"What's this, Eddie? Ventriloquism?"

"Because we aren't gonna make it as hoofers unless we diversify our act. Every night while I died of heatstroke in here, I've been practicing throwing my voice for you. I'm plain worn out, and I'm getting hoarse, but I wanted to surprise you. I didn't want you to see me fail if I couldn't do it. Whenever you came in, I'd hide him in the closet. You didn't like it by yourself in there, did you, Vincento?"

"How would *you* like it in there, you dummy?" said the dummy.

"That's great, Eddie. Your lips didn't move at all when you made him talk."

"*I* do the talking in this duo, lady," said the dummy.

"Oh yeah?" Eddie said.

"Yeah," the dummy said, Eddie making its head pivot from side to side, then once all the way around.

"Yikes, I'm getting dizzy," the dummy said.

"Knock on wood," my husband said, rapping his knuckles on the dummy's head.

"I feel unwanted when you do that," the dummy said.

"I know the feeling," I said to the dummy.

"You won't know it much longer, Ethel," Eddie said.

The next thing I know, two wooden arms are around me, a dummy is whispering "*C'est si bon,*" and I'm thinking I'm about to be ravished by a piece of lumber.

"Slide your hand in back of him," Eddie was telling me. "That way, by controlling his movements, you make him do what you like having him do."

As Eddie helped me out of my dress, I heard the dummy whispering, "*Bésame mucho,*" when he saw what lay beneath. As I stepped out of my red slip, he couldn't keep his eyes off me. I heard a gurgle in his throat.

"Oh, Eddie, are you sure it's okay to undress in front of him? We'll wear the poor dear out," I said.

"That's what he's here for. He's indestructible," Eddie said.

So this was Eddie Cohen, my strongman with the blond hair he touched up from time to time to bring out its highlights. He and Vincento did everything for me that night. I told Eddie I loved him with renewed fervor. I thanked him and the dummy for worrying about the future, said we'd get by, especially since there were three of us now. Before we made love again, Eddie put the dummy away. "Lemme out of here!" I could hear Vincento yelling from inside the closet. That's how far Eddie could throw his voice, but that dummy saved our marriage, so I didn't mind the interruption.

· · ·

We danced better than ever after that. When we next went to Cleveland, then Toledo, the dummy would whisper to me, "I can't wait to get you alone. Are you wearing the red slip?" Providence and New Haven audiences made the dummy and my husband come out for encores. We killed 'em in the "Borscht Belt" with Jackie Mason on the programme. At Niagara Falls and in the Poconos, we couldn't go out of our rooms without honeymooners asking the secret of our marriage.

"Talk to *him*," I'd tell them, pointing to Vincento, who would say, "A hard man is good to find."

"He's wood, but he sure can move," I'd say.

By the mid-'50s, I feared the dummy would turn into sawdust I used him so much. We were *all* worn out because my husband, once aroused, would follow the dummy. I guess it was what the French called a "*ménag—*" I don't know, something with menagerie in it. Vincento would look at me, roll his eyes. A big smile creasing his face, his head would flop down with exhaustion. Now showing his age, Eddie would fall asleep right behind him.

"It's been a wild ride, boys," I'd tell them as I watched their slumbers. Even *I* finally said no to them in Philly. I think the dummy was relieved. Eddie was for certain. Eddie'd ask, "How much can one man take?" From his perch, the dummy would smile at us. If I'd ever doubted Eddie's love, I didn't anymore. Vincento had given new vigor to us and our careers, but enough was enough.

I realized this the week we played the Block in East Baltimore. Back in our hotel room after a "Red Hot Rambler Show" at the Alcazar, I watched Eddie put the dummy on his lap. "Vincento, make me feel wanted. *Bésame mucho*," I said. I heard a groan. (A boat whistle down on the waterfront, I told myself.) "Make me feel your desires, Vincento. Say '*bésame mucho*' to me. Say 'Kiss me, Ethel Cohen.'"

They both said it, Eddie and Vincento, and the boys tried their darndest to satisfy me that night in Baltimore, for which I'll give them credit. But after an hour and twenty minutes of me with my eyes closed whimpering, "*Bésame mucho*. That wood feels good," Eddie said, "No, we can't do it, Ethel. We're old and tuckered out." The time had come, I knew, for a phased retirement from the conjugal bed.

• • •

Just a little (though not too much) past our prime now, we have a few rooms in Cincinnati, of all places. For cleaning ashtrays, scraping chewing gum off of floors and carpets, and sweeping and dusting halls and stairways, we get a break on the rent and a flat in the back of the fourteenth floor. The place advertises itself as "A Hotel of Dignity and Quiet Refinement—Famous for Large, Light, Airy Rooms." When the elevator's out of order and Eddie lugs the Bissel sweeper up the stairs, it ain't such a deal, he says. Thank heavens we never travel anymore; riding the elevator is a trip enough. It's a long way down to the street. Say the elevator's out, or say I've gone to pay a bill or to pick up sequins or feathers for the outfits. At each landing of the "Hotel of Quiet Refinement," I catch my breath, stare out the window, wonder why should we, Eddie and Ethel, The Dancing Couple (which we'd later changed to "The Makin' Whoopee Trio") clean windows when the manager never comes higher than the ninth floor to inspect our work? My face looks like Eddie's in the dirty windows. When we tap dance these days, more and more our faces look like Vincento, the dummy's: Thinning hair, eyes sunk in their sockets, rouge deep in the crevices of our cheeks.

There Eddie stands in the canary-colored jacket he works with on "Little Brown Jug" or "On the Sunny Side of the Street"—yes, there stands *my* Eddie! Wearing his pants with the black velvet stripes frayed around the pockets and his dancing shirt that's yellow around collar and cuffs, he rolls the Bissel into the corner. Shimmying, he hits me with a Tampa, tapping out the beat on the linoleum.

Dressed like that, his face and hands red from the heat lamp he sits under mornings, he says, "Watch your Eddie. Ready to see him dance?" On his face the wrinkles of seventy-one years collapse about his mouth and chin, sag downward. Everything—chin, chest—settles toward the dancing feet in patent leather shoes.

I nod to him. The room grows silent, not much in here but the nicked-up coffee table, a dresser, a foldaway cot. Eddie looks at the green paint peeling from the ceiling, counts to four, gives me a step or two, then backs up.

"Whew, I gotta sit," he says, falling down on the broken foldaway. "I'm out of breath."

I wonder how much I contributed to his condition over the years. I'll say this, he's still good to me. From the fourteenth floor, with Eddie resting, I watch and listen as our lives go by, mine, his, the dummy's life, who I suppose is ageless. As Eddie and Vincento sleep, I wonder where our stage careers are heading. We've got a matinee today.

A few minutes later, Eddie stirs again on the foldaway. Noontime shadows creep through the window. "Musta practiced too hard. I'm ready now, though. Fully recovered," he mumbles.

When he gets up, he looks better. He looks great! So do I in my gown with blue sequins, my pink earrings, my pink headdress.

"Watch me," he says. He adjusts his waist cinch. He brushes the creases from his canary jacket. "I'm stepping over in front, Ethel . . . hopping on the right foot, stepping back, gliding, sliding. Brush-step, ball-change."

"Just a minute. I'll hook myself in. It's not windy out so I'll just wear the headdress and throw a coat over my shoulders in the elevator."

I kiss the dummy with the dreamy smile still on his face, sit him in the window where he likes to be.

We dance down to the elevator, do a Shim-Sham as we enter it, do a Break, Wind and Unwind the Clock when we exit in the lobby. The manager says, "Did you sweep your floors with the Bissel?"

"We did, *mon ami,*" Eddie says. "Now it's show time."

I love Eddie's style, his *chutzpah* even with the manager. That's Eddie Cohen. You don't know him, but no one does a scuff-hop like Eddie. At the Roxy with an orchestra, me in blue chiffon with pink feather headdress, him in his canary coat; it's me for him and him for me.

We practice out in the alley to limber up. Noisy city traffic, people hurrying by all over. The gray hotel rises beside us, pigeons roosting on all twenty floors in front of the dirty windows. I see the dummy looking down, lonely for his dream girl.

Standing here, I do a Double Seven, Eddie humming, "Ta-cha . . . ta-cha-cha. . . ." A line of cars zips past out on the street.

On a Cincinnati sidewalk, Eddie Cohen hits me with a Cabriole; he insinuates me, syncopates me, travels sideways, taps out. "Be careful," he says. When I think he's gonna step into the path of an oncoming truck, he shimmies at the driver and breaks into a Front Essence.

"You goofy son-of-a-bitch, watch what you're doin'!" someone yells. Eddie shimmies harder. It's good to have a job in show business.

"You loved me, didn't you? In K.C., didn't you love me, Eddie?"

"Boy, didn't we love you," he says.

Most of the pink feathers of my headdress are matted together. Over my costume I wear a raincoat from the Next-to-New-Shoppe. Eddie gives me a Nelson Eddy stare.

"You might've forgotten in your old age, Ethel, but our aim is to create tap sounds that seem impossible to make when you think about them. How can I move this foot twice, see, and get four tap sounds outta two? It's the mystery and essence of tap dancing . . . more sounds, more clicks than there could possibly be moves for. It's an illusion of sound and sight just like ventriloquism."

"You loved me in Kansas City."

"Maybe we were making two sounds out of one back then," he says. "Wasn't it magical what we did?" He laughs, claps his hands, taps his feet. He still has that charm. The hair more gray than blond, the blue eyes, the wrinkled angles of forehead and cheeks—and that charm. Goddamn him for that charm!

"Ethel," he says, "here's the best joke of all." He makes me look at myself in a store window. He peers over my shoulder. Our two faces staring back are old but happy. "We've had good times, you, me, Vincento," he says just as someone yells, "Look at the old bastards," and cars speed by. "It's our meal ticket, what we do," Eddie says. "We're show people, troupers. It's in our blood. This is no worse than it was in Superior during the war years."

"It's the start of a new career, Eddie," I say. "I can feel it."

The crowds of workers coming out of the offices and stores for lunch clap when they see us. We wait three bars, then travel out. It's Limehouse Blues time, Cuban Pete time. They love us here on the street. They throw nickels and quarters in the shoe box at our feet.

"Shimmy for me, honey," Eddie whispers as the crowds go past. "Front Irish like Vincento is waiting for you, like your life depended on how good you shimmy."

"I am, Eddie," I say.

Jeezus, we're traveling now. Jeezus, we're going places.

A Philosophy of Dust

I, MICHAEL ZIMSKI, am a philosopher.

I needed my philosophical training when I got off a Superior Transit Authority bus at the end of the line one night last year. I'd quit a job as a garbage raker, moved to a new flat, and soon found my mailbox stuffed with unpaid bills. The night I waited by the docks for a bus, I turned middle-aged. I'd been drinking in a waterfront tavern, then at the Polish Club. At midnight, on the driver's last run, I rode out of this most broken-down part of Superior, Wisconsin.

"How can I get your job?" I asked the bus driver.

"Stay behind the yellow line," he said. "You're drunk. No talking to the driver."

At Belknap and Tower, no riders waited in the rain. At Belknap and Catlin, no midnight riders in the rain that had turned to snow. No riders clutching tokens in Central Park or in the East End and Allouez neighborhoods.

I got out when the bus driver stopped at the Choo-Choo Bar in the Itasca area of Superior. I watched him smoke a cigarette, stare at the night sky, then head back in the darkened bus to the bus barn on Winter Street.

That night last year—decades after I had left home for St. Louis, entered the seminary, went to school in Chicago, dropped out, started up again, got degrees in comparative literature and Slavic languages and literatures, after working a million places like Geno's Septic ("You Dump It, We Pump It") and Zenith Recycling as head garbage raker—I finally realized I had enough credits for a baccalaureate degree in Tough Living. Serenaded by empty boxcars being shunted in the railyard, I walked the two miles back to my childhood neighborhood to buy a six-pack before closing time at the Heartbreak Hotel.

The entire city of Superior, my neighborhood included, is a classroom for the study of failure. The curriculum for the Study and Analysis of Heartache comes from our citizenry's heavy drinking. We're Scandinavians, Slavs, and Indians of all makes and models. The curriculum is also tied to our living on the shore of the largest freshwater lake in the world. Lake Superior alters our weather for the worst, makes us ugly. Step out the door, see old newspapers blow down the streets in a lake wind, wipe dust from your eyes, go to the Palace Bar, Isle of Capri, Captain Cliff's Night Club, Lost in the '50s, Al's Waterfront Tavern. Find the locals lined up for an eye-opener at eight in the morning, and that, to a sensitive former academic like me, is Hard Knocks. When you can't find work and need to get yourself more depressed, listen in the hallway of your run-down flat for the neighbor guy to strike his wife or she him. Add gray skies. Add fog, and in winter and into late spring, throw in bitter cold, and that's how it is in Superior, Wisconsin, at the Head of the Lakes. Every day I take a refresher course in how to be a loser.

Now imagine a young man named Burr Orkit, employee of the Huron Cement Company. Given his humble job of delivering lime dust in a dusty place, you'd think he'd dwell on the meaning of life the way I did on the bus to the Choo-Choo Bar. I mean, here he is, a twenty-two-year-old delivering that which we will all come to eventually: Dust. But Burr, being carefree, does not think of mortality, of his place in the universe, or of other philosophical matters. He is a handsome guy. Six feet tall with good, sharp features, he'd walk up to you a little shyly, assuring you that you are okay with him no matter what. I always thought he resembled "the Polish James Dean," Zygmund Cybulski, star of Andrzej Wajda's movie *Popieł i diament* ... Ashes and Diamonds. With his looks, Burr has the same ability as Zygmund Cybulski to suggest an interior sadness. Over the months, he grew to be a beloved, dusty burr in this philosopher's side, I'll tell you.

I met him some time ago. I was in the Heartbreak Hotel having a beer when this young man beside me looked straight at himself in the mirror behind the bar and asked, "If I'm queer, wouldn't I think of men all the time when I reach organism?" He was a stranger and asking the question so I or anyone could hear.

"I don't know," I said. "All *I* think about is how to pay the rent. By the way, it's pronounced 'or-gasm.'"

"Just pondering things. I'm new here. I'm Burr Orkit. You look like you're pretty well set in life, mister. You've got a real nice house, I bet."

"Yes, I do." (It was a lie, since I was hard up for money and a month behind on the rent.)

"Where do you live? Where's your house? I'd rent a room from you."

"I live above us in an apartment," I said, pointing to a ceiling stained yellow from years of cigarette smoke.

Sometime during the four hours we spent drinking in the beer-and-smoke haze, I made him guess my line of work. "You're an insurance agent. A doctor. A high school music teacher. A choir director," he said.

"No, no, no," I said. "Better than that."

During a bathroom break, I gave myself a pep talk. "Confess to him what you do. He'll understand." Which I did when I got back to the bar.

"You're the district attorney," he said.

"Better yet," I said.

"What?"

"I'm a philosopher who waits on tables."

His jaw dropped, but we kept on sharing confidences. A few beers later, we confessed more things to each other—such as how often we attended Mass and whether we loved blondes better than brunettes.

"Just because I asked that about myself in the mirror, I'm not queer, ya know," he said.

"It's all right. This is the Heartbreak Hotel. In here we are what we say we are," I said.

"How 'bout this? My ex-girlfriend's in Pigeon Falls, Wisconsin. I haven't missed her for one second, and I've talked to a lot of girls in here and on the job already. I'm smart. I'm doing okay. One who comes in here that I've talked to is Marnie Hudacek. I'm not queer. I'm a fun seeker."

"Me, too," I said. "I'm no doctor or lawyer. I'm an intellectual. However, I confess that the intellectual you see before you overeats out of nervousness. At work I snatch a beet or a carrot off of diners' plates on the way from the kitchen to their table. Once I swiped a whole pork chop from Mrs. Pilsudski. When they're done eating and I'm clearing dirty dishes for Jan the dishwasher, I eat the leftover gristle and fat. I'm not health conscious. A hundred times a day I call orders back to the cook, 'Gimme the ham-and-egger, the roast beef plate, the *pierogi* special.'"

When Burr nodded encouragement, I continued my story. "I work in a Polish restaurant. I wear a Polish outfit to work. *Góral* wear them on special days in Poland. Did you know that *góral* means 'mountaineer' or 'highlander'? The costume has a flat hat with a partridge feather in it. Every day I put on a white shirt, a red vest with stitchery outlining a wild rose, red pants I can barely squeeze into anymore, white knee-length stockings. I wear black shoes, so this old pair of wingtips I have on suffices. See how the different gravies I've spilled have plugged up the holes in front? To be authentic I have to carry a mountaineer's walking staff. When I polka over to take an order, I say in Polish, 'Hi, I'm Michael. See the vest? I stitched the wild rose myself.'"

"Boy, that's the confession of a fun seeker," Burr Orkit said.

I bought him another beer and stared at myself in the mirror. Before I knew it, he handed me half a month's rent.

Let me say that in my eyes at least we became very serious roommates after our heartfelt confessions in the Heartbreak Hotel. Without wasting words, let me praise Burr Orkit. Let me dwell on him, on how his hair and eyebrows stood out to wonderful effect when he raided my closet to borrow my shirts with shades of purple and blue in them. If I could only see him in the Heartbreak wearing purple again, that Wal-Mart shirt! While we were roommates, he wore my T-shirts, too. He stood out from the other laborers around here.

• • •

But it is November now. I'm troubled trying to get at an aspect of that Burr, who had a special look. He had blue eyes that made him seem shy yet mysterious. The look was natural, forlorn, drawing you toward it. This is what women, and I, found irresistible. Young women (Marnie Hudacek), old women (Mrs. Schimanek, Mrs. Podhale)—they wanted to help him with his problem, though what it was, or if he even had a problem, no one really knew. It was the James Dean look, the Zygmund Cybulski look, that made him seem sensitive and troubled.

At six in the morning, as I filled the salt and pepper shakers at the Polish Hearth or licked the tip of my pencil to take a breakfast order, my troubled young roommate with the piercing blue eyes was yanking a tarp over the bed of a truck and preparing to head out to Litchke's place on County Road C to do a man's work. Once spread with lime and seeded, a field will produce good hay. The load Burr brought of hydrated lime helped neutralize the soil's acidity at Czerwinski's and Litchke's.

Burr was a traveler with dust, too. The company sent him to Eau Claire and to Minneapolis in a pneumatic truck, while I was stuck missing him in Nowhereville-by-the-Lake. There I stood in Polish costume, guest check in hand, as he delivered far and wide what remained after dolomite has been processed into pebble lime, hydrated lime, or the other kinds the Huron Cement Company ships out. He delivered his dust in Superior, too, to the men who bulldozed it into the white piles you see in hay country out on Polish Road.

Imagine Burr Orkit a part of the whiteness of lime. He *did* drive for his company. He *did* deliver dust. But this is no tragedy. I don't want to imply that a lime tragedy is imminent. Imminent instead is the story of a young man sitting alone on a county road that passes empty fields treated with the R K Fines or the hydrated lime he delivered a month before. As always, I sat at home waiting for him. It's my tragedy, if anyone's, I'm relating— the events of a life I should have prepared for but didn't, which leads to my renewed interest in philosophy and to such strange introspections that trouble me awake and asleep.

In my drafty apartment tonight, I keep thinking I've hurt and blinded people all my life . . . left them with the particles, the dust into which things disintegrate. For forty years I've served others the dust of my lost dreams, and now Mephistopheles comes up the stairs to the apartment where, walking staff parked in the closet, I, a never-married, overweight, fifty-five-year-old

Ph.D. in a *góral* outfit, sit in the gathering dusk. This, if ever, is the time for thinking, when Mephisto makes his rounds, when the dust-laden wind sweeps the lime-sweet hayfields, when the light snow glances on streetlights and settles along curbs, when the sky is a white razor to my black thoughts. What, dear God, is Burr Orkit doing while I cry alone at home tonight? Tell me how I've come to let my fingernails grow so long.

This lonely night I think how, discharged from the military years before, I got into spiritual trouble in a Catholic seminary, quit there to become the perpetual student like Peter Trophi-moff of *The Cherry Orchard,* then found work teaching high school. I quit after four years, left for Minneapolis, became a student again, studied Polish and Russian, gained admission to the "U," withdrew, reentered, exceeded the time limit for completing my dissertation, and finally—at age forty-nine, with balding head and graying sideburns—completed the dissertation and said to myself in Ukrainian, "*Proschaj i ne vertajsja* . . . Good-bye and don't come back." What I want to know is why I never stuck with anything in life? This is the theme of another introspection to which life with Burr has brought me: that I will always be served the dust of life, having it delivered to my door upstairs in the Heartbreak Hotel, where I sit alone in an unclean apartment.

· · ·

In these rooms above the bar with the neon HEARTBREAK sign, we, Burr and I, had a chair, a TV set, an end table with plastic drawer handles, a footstool for His Majesty King Burr, a floor lamp with a three-way bulb, a bookcase for my philosophy books—Bachelard, Habermas, Kierkegaard—and for the one tome Burr Orkit ever consulted: *A History of the Green Bay Pack-ers*. We had a noisy refrigerator, a stove, plywood cupboards. Except in the kitchen, which had yellowing linoleum, we had hardwood floors. I didn't mind cleaning the place if Burr would only shake out his clothes before coming in after work, to cut down a little on the dust. We got along fine, each of us happy to have someone there.

The building is one hundred years old. Natural light shines through the windows. The outside has brown wooden shingles and faces Fifth Street in the little East End. The roof of the Heartbreak Hotel slants backward from Fifth toward the alley. Burr and I had the front apartment. A merchant seaman named John Kalinowski and his wife once lived here. We'd find things he'd hidden (beneath the linoleum, a port pass for the Shatt al Arab ports in the Persian Gulf, directions for using a Sanitube for personal hygiene around the genitals). Two windows in our living room and the two in Burr's now-empty bedroom look out over the street. At night the neon HEARTBREAK sign colors the empty rooms.

So many girls came here when Burr and I were roomies that Burr could have used a Sanitube. I told him if he wasn't quiet in bed with his women, I wouldn't bring him leftovers from the café.

To hide my annoyance when he walked in with some new girl, I'd laugh. "*Nie odmawiaj sobie radośći . . .* Don't postpone joy," I'd say, then go to my room to imagine yet another hot babe rolling up *my* T-shirt on *his* sun-tanned chest, pulling it over his head and off of him, probably asking him, "Who *is* that odd fellow in the kitchen?"

Was the muffled sound Burr identifying me as his grandfather? Were they laughing at me?

Burr and women. The occasional thump against the wall during their casual evenings. His handsome face pushing into her bosom to smother his groans, so I, the grandpa in the next room, wouldn't hear them. The click of the door as she left. Once or twice a month a woman from uptown came to see if she could make Burr vulnerable to her. The visitors left lovestruck, but was Burr Orkit himself smitten? Never, not on your life. Burr'd wake up crabby for lack of sleep.

"Make me coffee," he'd say, stumbling into the kitchen. "What time she leave?"

"Three A.M."

Eyes red, chin rough with wheat-colored stubble, he'd sit in his underwear studying the weather. "I got a long day." He'd rub his face.

"When you get back, go to bed. Catch up on your sleep," I'd tell him.

"Didn't drink much, but I feel like shit. That one last night, her recipe took sixth place in something called the United Way of Greater Duluth Chili Cook-Off. Her name was Johanna. Hand me the coffee."

"Was she a sixth-place finisher?"

"I finished her five times."

That whole winter he went fun seeking. I know he was fun hunting that first year on Halloween and All Saints' Day, because I distinctly remember the diners talking about the All Saints' Day storm of 1968, when Superior got thirty-six inches of snow in two days. I was living in St. Louis with Donny Myron at the time. I know Burr Orkit was seeking fun on Veteran's Day '98, too, because I am a veteran and pay attention to the day. And during Advent he hunted fun, because I talked to him seriously about the propriety of doing so before Christmas. And on Valentine's Day, and on Easter Sunday, and on Memorial Day '99. He was a fun lover who'd go on and on without a thought for anyone but himself.

Then out of nowhere comes Rose Wahl. When he brought *her* home, it worried me. She was no also-ran, I can tell you. For a week he talked about her. "She's not from here. She works in the country putting in a pipeline. I got lucky. Never seen a woman so beautiful. I was delivering lime dust. I seen workers eating, smoking, taking it easy on lunch break. The truck says GREAT LAKES GAS TRANSMISSION. Zimmy [that was his pet name for me], are you listening to me? Rose was leaning on a tire of the truck. She wore a hardhat, safety vest, light blue shirt, blue jeans. You listening? For a minute she looked like a man."

"Listening. Is *your* heart listening, Burr?" I asked him.

"You know it is," Burr said. "Lemme tell you. I parked the lime truck. I stretched my legs. I made four trips by noon, then six or seven guys and a truck show up, and she's in the safety vest. The pipeline crew started in Alberta, Canada, and was now finally moving through Czerwinski's on the way to the Lakehead Refinery.

"'Can I get a drink from your water cooler?' I asked them.

"'Yes,' she said. Because her hair was pinned under her hardhat, I didn't know until she took it off that she was a woman. The paper drinking cups had messages and reminders. Mine read, 'Your Future Depends on Your Safety.' Above the message was a turbaned swami with his hands stretched over a crystal ball. 'Hey, my future depends on my safety.'

"Rose showed me her cup: 'Safety Is Your Own Look-Out,' it read. A solitary eye on the paper cup stared at me. 'These things are really funny,' I said."

"Please, Burr, you've told me this story before."

"I like to tell it," he said.

Since we'd become roommates, he had what he called fifth- and sixth-place women finishers, depending on how much he wanted to go to bed with them, once a tenth-place finisher named Maaret-Hanelle Laitala, a Finn. But I grew seriously troubled with his talk of Rose Wahl. I couldn't concentrate. At work I kept messing up orders. Harriet Bendis yelled at me for serving her pork hocks instead of pork sausages.

"I thought you were so bright with your smart talk," she said to me. I wanted to brain her with my *góral* walking staff. I was worried. If Burr moved out on me, what'd become of me? Where would my Polish James Dean go?

When I finally met Rose face to face, I found a lot wrong with her. She was no good for Burr. Much too tall a woman. Shoulders too broad. Though she worked on the pipeline crew, she pretended to be naive and pure. I didn't buy it. There was no accounting for *his* taste, though. When I was heating leftovers and he'd walk into the fluorescent light of the kitchen and say, "I ate supper with Rose," I wanted to tell him, "You can do better in a woman. I suppose you don't want my suppers now." On the days after an evening out with her, he'd eat whatever I was preparing, even chili, which he told me he hated. Then he'd go straight to bed.

My workdays were long. Dirty dishes came in all day at the café. The dust never stops at a cement plant on the waterfront. Neon signs blinked on in the windows of bars with names like Dreamland, Happyland, and the EZ Rider. In one of these, Burr would meet her, his Rose-Deep Well of Joy. Their first date was at Happyland. Happyland! Oh, they were so light-hearted, sitting in a booth confessing their secrets.

Bay City is far from here—in Michigan. That's where she, or where the company she worked for, was located. When she was here in the East End, she ate supper in the café. Always with Burr. When I wrote the order in the guest check, I'd say to him, "Then you won't be eating at home tonight with me?" She'd shake her head for him. "No," she'd say. "You'll excuse us both tonight."

Another night she gave me a souvenir paper cup. The two hands on it lay palm upward. "Your Safety Is Largely in Your Hands," read its message. Looking at it, I wished my safety *were* in my hands. I fell asleep to the sounds of the jukebox downstairs playing all the old songs. I was losing Burr to Rose, who this very evening was in my kitchen playing cards.

When I awoke to "Heartbreak Tango," I knew they were spinning, twirling, dancing downstairs in the bar, my roommate and the girl.

I'll not deny she was beautiful to him and, I suppose, to a few others. She was also a woman practicing safety, which may explain her sitting aloof from the other workers when Burr met her, for by then she'd had enough of the talk you can only imagine from a crew of pipeline workers.

When free of the hardhat, her hair—the yellow of aspen leaves in September—fell to her shoulders. In the Heartbreak's dusky light, her hair shone, her eyes sparkled. The sun over the pipeline had darkened her skin. I won't say much else of her except that Burr Orkit, not being safety conscious, fell in love, whereupon he began worrying about the transitory nature of pipeline work. "If she goes, she goes," I told him. "Don't give up being a fun seeker on account of her."

When she telephoned and Burr wasn't in, I told her some things about him, too. "You know he likes his fun, Rose," I said. "Whether with you or with me . . . it doesn't matter. He likes and needs it. He's a normal boy."

"What kind of fun does he have with you?" she asked.

"You know," I said.

"I bet you two go to movies and play Scrabble. I bet you watch football games," she said.

"*You* know, Rose," I said again.

"You fight over the sports page, right? You yell scores back and forth. You tell each other sports trivia."

"No, Burr's more advanced than that," I told her. "He's a free-wheeling, natural lad who takes fun where he can find it," I said.

"Fun like sitting in bars, like shooting pool, and meeting girls?" said Rose. "That's what pipeline guys do."

"Men do other things. They lay pipe in dark places."

"What do you mean?" said Rose.

"I don't want to hurt anyone's feelings, but in terms of fun seeking, I'm kind of a father figure to Burr. He comes in when he doesn't get any from you and tells me about it. Then I advise him. This will hurt your feelings, but I relieve him of the tension buildup you have caused him. He's uncertain afterward. He's always worrying. I tell him a pipe, any type of pipe, has two ends, and he can have and work both."

"Not with me he won't," she said, her voice rising. "I don't believe you."

"You may know him better, but I know I'm right. I know what we have. I know how he wants it." It was all lies, but it worked. The night the pipeline crew pulled out, their work over, Marnie Hudacek, a Heartbreak Hotel regular, called me from the bar downstairs. "He's getting drunk down here," she said.

Smudged black from the dust and smoke in the autumn sky, the moon rose large as the jukebox played "Heartbreak Tango." Either the record was stuck, or Burr himself was playing it over and over on purpose. I didn't know why he was drinking more than usual, but I hoped if it had to do with Rose leaving, we could now establish a routine, just the two of us, like before.

At three in the morning, I heard a commotion—Burr coming into the apartment, trying to find his bed. The hum of my bedside clock kept me awake. The dusty moon set. How was Burr feeling? As if my own heart hadn't broken those nights he danced the tango with Rose Wahl.

A minute later I heard him step into my room.

"Burr?"

"She left," he said in a voice barely louder than the hum of the clock.

In the black shadow of the door, I saw a white T-shirt. "Here. Can you find a chair? Do you need help?" I asked him.

"I'm pretty drunk."

"Do you want me to heat leftovers?"

"She left. I was— Did you say something to her?" he asked.

"No, Burr."

"The truck Czerwinski spread lime dust on his fields with is always unlocked behind the lime piles. We used to sit in there, Rose and me. We looked out at his fields and dreamed. No one could see us. Did you say something to her? A day ago, I was goofing around. I was asking her the question I asked you at the bar that time we met: If I'm queer, wouldn't I be thinking of men during an organism, an orgasm . . . whatever you call it? When she jumped down from the truck, I said to her, 'What're you doing? Where are you going?' I could see her face had changed. She yelled something back at me, called me a fun seeker with two sides to me."

"You better rest," I said, trying to calm him. "You better eat leftovers. You know I like Rose."

"The guys laughed when I went out there and asked if Rose went back to Michigan. 'Your safety is your own look-out,'" Burr said. "But my safety's in *her* hands. She has no phone number. Her pipeline won't give it out. Did you say anything to her about me? I've been drinking so long I can't stand up."

Inching sideways along the wall, he made it into the kitchen for a beer. It must have been four o'clock. Head bobbing up and down, he was sobbing, "'Knowledge plus Caution equals Safety!' My safety record's horseshit." His head fell to the side. Back in the room, he stumbled over to the old *góral*. I slipped out of my red-beaded vest with its intricate design of a wild rose and tried to comfort him the only way I knew how.

He awoke at noon sick of heart. With only a few hours' sleep, I was tired myself, yet happy. Rose was gone. No bothersome fragrance left in Superior. I hoped we'd never see her again.

When I came in from grocery shopping, I wondered what Burr recalled of the night before. He was pale.

"How'd I get in your bed?" he asked.

"I slept out on the davenport," I answered.

"Is it a workday?"

"I called in an excuse for you."

"I'm gonna be sick. Gimme a paper bag or something to throw up in," he said.

Downstairs, World War III was beginning. Oh, how they turn up that jukebox! When Ed, the owner, steps out, the other bartender lets people do whatever they please. I knew from the music that "Gob" Goligoski was quarreling with old lady Sniadyak, just as I would know that Earl Malkowski was in the bar when "Cross Over the Bridge" played one hundred times. When Gob punched a Whoopee John Wilfahrt tune, D-7, Mrs. Sniadyak got up from the booth along the back wall and played F-9, "Harper Valley PTA." Spiteful people get to you. D-7. F-9. D-7. F-9. I'd go crazy if I heard them again, I thought, and pounded my *ciupaga,* my walking staff, on the floor.

When I did, Burr shouted, "Oh, my head. Don't do that!" Then he got sick all over the blankets. "Take care of me, will you?"

I held him while he turned from pale to green. He was so sick I think his lost flower came only dimly and fleetingly to mind. You cure a hangover before you cure a heart. I changed his blankets, then made lunch and rested.

Burr slept away the afternoon. At five, he muttered her name. At six, he ate a cracker, sipped leftover soup. At seven, he got up for a beer. "I'm shaky," he said.

"I'll get us through," I said.

"What happened last night?"

"You hurt bad. I felt awful for you. Couldn't you love someone else?"

"What?"

"Do you want another beer?"

"Yes."

"Could you love someone as much as I could, Burr? Is that impossible for you?"

He didn't know what I meant. Still, I thought to myself, he must remember my healing touch if only dimly. I think he remembered it but let the Rules of Safety and Self-Preservation keep him from dwelling on it. If he recalled my healing touch, then what? What would he think of himself? Now was the time for playing a man's game, now before he got more and more frantic over a beautiful pipeline worker.

After he dressed, in the moment before he opened the apartment door, he whispered "Wild Rose," which I knew was admitting he remembered my red vest of the night before.

· · ·

Nights, after working all day in the lime truck, Burr Orkit now lay in our apartment stunned. No woman walked out on Burr, who in the bars was a preferred customer because of his good looks and drawing power with women. Because he was heartbroken for the first time, I knew he needed the extraordinary measures of an old custom. Who knows from what folk wisdom or superstition this custom arose? The placing of a fish over Burr Orkit's heart, the old treatment of centuries back, came a few days later. On nights when neither of us slept well and he'd wake me to give him something for his broken heart, the fish that resembles an eel, I'd say, "Shh—Close your eyes then." Placing a damp washcloth on his forehead, I'd sing, "*Zasiali górali, żyto, żyto,*" which means "the mountaineers sowed rye." "That's us, that's you and me, Burr—Polish highlanders looking for roses."

According to custom, you skin the fish, dry the skin, and

bury the skinned fish together with the fish skin in the earth overnight before applying only the skin—this is important, *only* the skin—to the chest of the broken-hearted. Instead, I placed the whole fish, body, skin, and head, lengthwise, running it from Burr's collarbone to his heart. I turned it the other way around sometimes so the old, dead eye of the fish stared back at me, the old intellectual.

When I suggested he roll over so I could continue his cure, he said, "Just don't leave. Stay here with me while I close my eyes."

"Feel the fish on your chest then. Feel it soaking in. You're going to be better. It's only been a few days, not even a week, and this custom is very old, so it's bound to work," I reassured him.

Being in that room was torture for me when my life depended on pleasing Burr Orkit. A singing mountaineer, I started to lose weight. And Burr wasted away. You'd think he was Ivan Denisovich in the gulag. I wondered how he delivered dust in his weakened condition.

"When I first laid eyes on her," he'd tell me, "I never saw anyone so beautiful."

"Do you *have* to tell me this again? It's four o'clock. Go to sleep. She's left town."

If he wouldn't stop his lament for Rose Wahl, I'd lay my head below the tail of the fish and say, "My future depends on your safety." As he talked he'd rest his hand in my hair. With me now sharing his room, he'd forget she'd gone to Michigan. He had the messages to read from his drinking cups and someone to hear him say it wasn't his fault she'd gone. Then he fooled himself into thinking she wasn't gone.

There is the suggestion of great, tragic love in all of this. So sick with sorrow, how could he know, in a dark room, which was the intentional sigh and which the accidental, as I lay the lingfish on him and the radiator hissed and spit out water from its valve? Bare-chested, he waited for me, for the interpreter of the old custom, to roll up his T-shirt to apply the remedy. "Rose . . . oh my Rose," he'd say.

Wearing the red-beaded vest, I'd say, "Awake, Alert, Alive."

"Knowledge plus Caution equals Safety," he'd say. "Rose?"

"Yes, Burr," I'd say, "that's my name on this night of old memories, your Wild Rose."

• • •

Then her scent. It returned in the form of telephone calls that a drunken Burr never knew about. "He's not home," I'd tell her. "He left town. He's with Marnie Hudacek, and they're *not* at Happyland."

"Will you tell him I miss him?" Rose pleaded.

"It'll do no good, because I won't see him. You're aware of his drawing power. He's exploring other options," I said.

After several more calls with Rose breaking down when I told her he was exploring other options, the calls ceased. So, you see, in the end Rose Wahl was just a quitter; a few lies from me and she quit on him.

The formerly fun-seeking trucker grew weaker and weaker. The black mark of worry colored his eyes. That's when I should have introduced Mephistopheles to him. It's interesting how the first scent of loneliness makes certain people change. This was a different side of Burr from the mysterious star side. Here was God's lonely soul in the apartment on East Fifth.

From that time on, everything we did was for Burr's benefit and mine. When we talked about Rose all night, in the shadows I was Rose and he was Burr; then he was Rose and I was Burr. In the morning he'd forget. He put me in charge so he could forget. I took charge.

Then he didn't trust me. On a night after a month and a half of wasting away and drowning in my shirts, he asked me, "Is this philosophy?"

"Yes," I said. "Nihilism."

Neither Burr's voice nor his face, but his eyes, said to me, "I was stabbed by a Rose. I know you said something to her."

There was a sudden shock of recognition in Burr Orkit's eyes. Why the sudden change, why the clear sight when there was around us a paradise of dreams—the color of evening in our rooms, the downstairs jukebox, the healing touch of me as his Wild Rose?

"I trusted you," he said. Over and over he said it like it was the tango "Jalousie" playing on and on. I pretended not to hear.

"Let's try the fish," I said.

"I trusted you. I'm not a two-way fun seeker," he told me.

As I looked about for the stinking lingfish, he said tomorrow he was heading to Czerwinski's lime piles.

"What are you going to find out there that's better than right here?"

"Something . . . anything. Maybe some different roses."

The next day I thought how foolishly Burr was blaming me for everything. Loneliness is a cold wind in the chambers of an empty heart. People do almost anything to warm that lonely room. Burr did. Why should *I* suffer for that?

I made it through breakfast and lunch shifts. At home in my uniform, I took a break. For ten minutes I sat on Burr's footstool when, believing I heard Mephistopheles, I opened the apartment door to find Burr.

"Don't come in with all that dust on you. Shake it off first."

"I'll shake *you* off all right," he said, pushing me aside.

"What, Burr?"

"I know what you've been doing. Goddamn, I'd kill you if I

hadn't had the good luck to fall for someone like Marnie Hudacek."

"Let's sow rye together, highlander."

"No more highlands. No more. You lied. I was out at Czerwinski's. If you tell anyone about that fish you put on me— I hate you."

"Of course you'll hate me if you can't love. You've seen, maybe in the mirror in the lime truck, what roses do. But please sow rye with me tonight."

His face whitened. "You old tub! You don't make any sense," he shouted. "I musta been drunk all these months. You're a crazy, pathetic fatman. I should stab you! I looked in the mirror all right. It showed me to get away from *you*, Fatso. No thanks to anything I learned from you, I have a new rose, Marnie. You better stay away from Marnie and me."

He grabbed my *ciupaga*. I cried, "No, not that!" His face growing icy, he smashed the walking stick over his knee.

"Go to work with *these*!" he said, throwing the two pieces at me. "Use them as canes, you goddamn loser."

He snatched my hat with the partridge feather and stomped on it as well. I was in tears.

"I'm praying for you," I said. "Listen, 'In the beginning was the Word, and the Word was God—,'" but before I could reshape the hat, he was gone through the heavy door.

I looked for him. I saw Mrs. Sniadyak stumble into the Heartbreak as Gob Goligoski stumbled out. Back at work, I stared hopefully from the kitchen when customers entered. At four-fifteen, Mrs. Bendis and her sodality crew stopped in. They looked at my gravy-stained wingtips, then talked about my premature baldness. I could only lean forward on the two short sticks Burr'd made of the *ciupaga*. My heart was an empty room. I didn't hear a thing the ladies ordered.

"Zimski," they asked after ten minutes, "where's supper? We have sodality meeting."

"I'll get you a stinking fish fry," I said. "I'll serve you anything. How about used fly paper? How about the bowl-of-grease special with ant cups for dipping? The main entrée is shit. Don't know if there'll be enough. Jan's been bound up lately." Hearing them gasp at my recitation of tonight's dinner specials, hearing the bell over the café door tinkling as I opened it, I hobbled out of the Polish Hearth forever.

That's when I saw the bus had left from the safety zone on East Fifth and that I had become the cripple of my last introspection, which was on love and why I've never found it. With a weak soul and a crushed heart, I walk with two canes now. In my guest check, I write my last order over and over: Burr Orkit. Burr Orkit. Burr Orkit.

• • •

Now the icy streets stab me. Right through my flabby belly I feel them. Into my heart cuts this white razor of nihilism.

Listen! Mephisto's turning his key. I gave it to him as part of a deal. Hear his breathing? See the door shake slightly?

In the minute before the door opens, let me confess I gained back my weight plus an additional fifteen pounds when Burr ran off with Marnie Hudacek. They went to North Dakota and returned in a week, married. When I encountered them at the fish market, he said it again, "I should stab you."

It got worse. The next time I saw them (broken-hearted, I was hobbling along on my canes) he pretended not to notice me. His avoiding me wounded my soul. I hurried home to my empty rooms above the Heartbreak. Crazy, broken-hearted me, I banged my canes on the floor and pounded my feet when someone laughed or the jukebox came on downstairs. After a day of this, the bartender telephoned. "Cut it out, Zimski," he said.

"You're causing a disturbance." He said I was also a visual disturbance for the way I looked these days. I banged the telephone
receiver on the wall.

An hour later, a policeman who'd been listening undercover
downstairs came upstairs, banged on my door, and handed me a
ticket. "I'm disorderly in my conduct because my thoughts are
disordered," I told him. When he left, I pounded again. Rose had
killed Burr, and Burr had killed me. Now he'd kill Marnie
because he couldn't truly love after Rose. This was something to
make noise about. What's left for Burr Orkit? What's left for
Michael Zimski, crippled with canes? Nothing but dreadful
sounds in the night, dread of an hour when they stop, dread of a
night when the neon HEARTBREAK HOTEL sign goes out and the
sign stands in darkness.

In these last weeks and hours of a waning century comes the
devil. I have my canes ready. At twenty-three years of age, Burr
Orkit sits alone in someone else's truck parked behind a mountain of lime while his youthful bride eats a bowl of buttered
popcorn at home and watches *The Maury Povich Show.* I've traded Mephisto to know these things about them. In the end, isn't
this how we all go, married, unmarried, young or old—hidden
from others, broken-hearted, dreading the close of day, dreading
the last mile, the final receipt? Burr got enlightened in a lime
truck. I've become enlightened, too. All day and night the jukebox is stuck on a new one: "Who Put the Bop in the Bop-Shu-
Bop-Shu-Bop—?" I go on pounding.

With the palms of my dirty hands, I pull down a window
shade to hide myself from God. *He's* the One Who put the bop
in the bop-shu-bop. My fingernails are so long and curved I
can't do much at all with my hands. I can't go to work. Who'd
order from a waiter with filthy nails and yellow teeth? I sit in
darkness all day and stare at the vase of roses by the phone. Rose

Wahl sent them to Burr Orkit from Michigan. I wait for eviction. I wear my waiter's uniform. I'll leave in style when my time comes. The vest is stained. The shirt stinks. Dead roses blacken in a vase. "*Zasiali górali, żyto, żyto.*" I hum "The Eviction Waltz." Oh, Burr, You Beautiful Highlander, didn't you know I could have helped you through it? Oh, if you'd let me, I could have fixed it all right for us, Burr.

I would have made our suppers.

I would have done the washing.

I would have taken three jobs and given you my tips. I'd have wrapped you in such fine fish skins.

The Value of Numbers

IN THE NAVY HOSPITAL in Yokosuka, Japan, Tad Milszewski's broken leg was reset, his ribs taped, his head bandaged. The rifle company's lieutenant, who'd witnessed the accident outside DaNang, recommended Lance Corporal Milszewski for the Purple Heart, which would be awarded him before he left Japan to complete his recuperation in the United States.

Alone in the dark hospital room, the youthful marine felt embarrassed about the Purple Heart, knowing people would laugh when they learned what had caused the wounds that would keep him on crutches so long. He was a cook riding in the back of a deuce-and-a-half when it went off one of the old French highways, leaving him pinned beneath two washtubs and a field stove. He'd get through this, he thought, turning his attention to the nurse who'd give him his hypo. Under her watchful eye, he solved many problems that had vexed him the past five nights, such as had he done enough for his country in Vietnam and should he be embarrassed that the lieutenant's men went without a hot meal because of the accident?

When the nurse found him lifting his leg as part of his therapy, she said, "Good for you, Milszewski. Keep at it. You'll be cooking in no time."

He counted aloud each time he elevated the shattered leg, switching to Polish after awhile. Far from home, where better to find comfort than in his parents' language? He counted, prayed, then muttered, "*Jest to piękna noc . . .* This is a beautiful night" or "*Tysiące gwiazd błyszczą na niebie . . .* Thousands of stars glitter in the sky." He said "*brat i siostra,*" too, "brother and sister."

At age nineteen, Lance Corporal Milszewski was learning certain ironies of life. One of them was that seven years before, his sister, whose name the family pronounced "Ah-nya," the Polish way, also lay in a hospital recovering from an operation on her leg and later was sent home to recover in their East End neighborhood of Superior, Wisconsin. *Five days in Yokosuka and no letter from Anna, he thought. Now that she's better, why won't she write me?*

Drifting in and out of fevered sleep, he remembered their dad rigging up a contraption in her room. A piece of cloth served as a sling. From it a wire cord rose to a pulley fixed to the ceiling. The cord looped over the top of the pulley then down to a metal bar with two sand-filled bags hanging from it. The bags and the bar provided a counterweight to the pressure Anna would exert on the sling with her leg.

"Make the bags *ri-y-ce* toward the ceiling," their father said to her in broken English. After seven years, Thaddeus could hear their voices plainly, the father counting in Polish "*Jeden,*" the sister responding "One," the bags rising toward the ceiling.

"*Dwa.*"

"Two."

"*Trzy.*"

"Three."

When his parents weren't upstairs with her, his grandmother, whom they called Babusia, the aunts, or certain St. Adalbert's rosary sodality ladies were caring for Anna—Mrs. Sniadyak, Mrs.

Adjukiewicz, Mrs. Pilsudski. Because everyone wanted to make Anna Milszewska better, two languages got mixed up in the house—the way they did now when he said, "I need something to help me sleep," but, confused, told the nurse in Polish, "It's cold in here." Knowing what the wounded need, the nurse said, "I'll be right back with your shot."

He remembered he'd been assigned certain times to sit with Anna, who was a year younger than he. "*Brat i siostra . . .* brother and sister." When he wanted to be playing with friends or be down by the bay spying on the two herons that stood motionless in the shallows, he was watching his sister for an hour and a half each spring evening until the day she was strong enough to walk. He never went into her room other times. Now in Japan he recalled her room's beige wallpaper, the bed with the walnut frame, the brown linoleum curling along the edges of the floor. He'd hated the word *polio,* hated that it was *their* house with someone sick in it. He hated to see his ma go around the neighborhood with a canister asking for money for polio research, hated to see Babusia carrying pans of water upstairs to wash her granddaughter's hair, hated the way the theater stopped movies halfway through so Greer Garson on screen could request that donations be given the ushers passing by. Everyone in the place knew they were donating a dime or nickel to help Tad Milszewski's sister and a handful of other East End kids with polio.

When he entered her room for his evening shift, Anna would turn her head on the pillow, tighten her lips. She knew he was embarrassed by her condition. After five minutes, he'd say, "You should see what I did today. I went to Petroski's house. They're building a garage. Then me and Bob Kiszewski walked to the river to see if anyone was fishing." There ended the conversation, replaced by the scent of lilacs rising through the screen window or by the sound of their mother's clematis scraping the side of the trellis below in the spring breeze. Between them a scent of lilacs, a scraping of vines. Brother and sister.

He read to her from a book: "Herons and bitterns belong to a large order, which includes many notable birds such as the egrets, Maribou storks of Africa and India, and others equally as interesting."

"*Jeden*," she'd say when he did this. She'd force her leg down against the weight of the sand in the bags, counting in Polish.

When she got to ten or eleven repetitions and began counting in English, he stopped reading and said, "You can't go past *that* in Polish? I bet you've never seen a heron either." Then he added, "How could you see the herons when you can't walk?" "It's not important," she said, moving her Wards Airline radio closer to the bed. Those days she was like a distant song on a faraway station.

Now he, Tad Milszewski, was far away from home and his leg ached. When it did, he resented the way she'd acted seven years before—as though he wasn't in her room, as though he was invisible to her.

"You were talking about your sister," the nurse said.

"It's been five days. Why doesn't she write?"

"She will. I imagine she doesn't know you're here. Can you hold off a minute more on the medication? I'll be right back," the nurse said.

"I can't hold off. She hasn't written."

He stared at the ceiling, the curtains, what he could see of the shiny tile floor of the hallway. Drumming his fingers along the edge of the hospital bed mattress, he recalled the sun setting behind the corner turrets of the East End fire hall, behind the chimneys of the Northern Block building, behind the Euclid Hotel. Another spring evening without seeing the herons because of his sister, and he was getting nervous about the pain now. He had hated being ashamed of her, but he couldn't help himself. It was hard to go out of the house because of the shame. It was hard to have a Purple Heart, given the way he'd earned it.

When the hospital quieted, the yelling of the wounded stopping, when there was no sound in the hallway now, only a dim light on and the nurse hurrying back and forth, he began to think a little differently about Anna. Especially as time grew near for the nurse's return, he listened carefully in his mind for the sound of weights and a pulley in his sister's room. Over and over, alone in stillness, he whispered about Anna to the blue herons from his boyhood, telling them how beautiful his sister was to him in his hour of need, how really beautiful tonight was going to be, how easily he could count to ten in Polish despite his injured leg. He'd count higher if the nurse hurried.

At midnight, he was calling out each time he elevated his leg an inch. "*Jeden, dwa, trzy,*" he was saying through the pain, realizing with each number what he'd been afraid of admitting: that Anna Milszewska, though younger and stricken with polio, was still stronger than her brother Thaddeus, who was now clamoring for his medication.

"This will help," said the navy nurse when she heard him pleading with her to hurry, as though the medicine she brought could help him forget what he'd said to his sister about the herons years before.

"Where were you?" he asked her when he'd counted to a hundred.

"You'll be all right. You'll sleep. This'll fix you up," said the nurse.

It took only a moment.

Before he drifted off, he wanted to ask her if she'd seen the blue herons by the bay, but the nurse left quickly. There was still no letter from Anna either, telling him she wasn't embarrassed about his wounds. But there were a few things she'd left him to get through the night—the Polish numbers, the scraping of clematis vines on the trellis, the good scent of her hair after Babusia had washed it.

Leokadia and Fireflies

NAMED STEFANIE Karawinska, I'm seventeen years old. The woman in the title of the story, Sister Mary Leokadia, is perhaps fifty. Because the nuns at my grade school here in Superior wear black habits and white, scarflike wimples covering their hair and ears, I can't tell their ages. They belong to an order founded for Polish and Polish-American women: the Sisters of St. Joseph of the Third Order of St. Francis, whose main convent is in Stevens Point, Wisconsin, where I'd stop on the way to Milwaukee if it weren't far out of the way.

Though this story is about my family and principally about my dad and has only a little to do with Sister Leokadia, I'm still naming it for her. Because the nuns do so much for us, and yet remain in the background of our lives, credit is due them. I'm entering Marquette University in the fall partly because of the nuns. Though after attending Szkoła Wojciecha, St. Adalbert's grade school, I went to a public high school, I'd see the nuns in church; they'd have me do odd jobs for them at school, and sometimes Sister Leokadia would visit our house. Because she's a holy presence in the neighborhood, this story is named for her, the nun who taught me in seventh and eighth grades.

I'd never name a story for myself. I shouldn't even use *I* so much, but how else to describe yourself when you're a character in your story? I have medium-length light-brown hair with bangs. In back, my hair is straight, trimmed evenly across. I wish I were as pretty as Mother. I try to be modest in speech and dress, to read a lot, to study writing in the months before college. A tall girl, I blush when teased. I have pale skin. Who isn't pale in June with winter not long over in northern Wisconsin? I wear glasses for all the reading I do. A photo of Stefanie Karawinska, author and minor character in this, her family's story, would show an average girl, plain in appearance, which is true.

I live with my parents and Dziaduś, Grandfather, a retired seaman in poor health, in a house in the East End. So you'll know both the heredity *and* the environment that shape my life, I'll describe the two lower floors of our house, starting with a basement, where dust webs catch on thin plastic window curtains. In the basement fourteen years ago, Dad built plywood cabinets. The basement—which during other seasons is damp and cool—during winter is the warmest place in the house, for in the center stands a furnace converted to burn natural gas. Tin vents rise through the house, carrying warm air to us up here, too. Along with the basement workbench and the furnace are the washing machine, laundry tub, scrub board, and the old coal bin, now made into a storage room. Sometimes even on Memorial Day, the furnace comes on.

Most of our time is spent upstairs, where the cabinets Dad built hang above the sink on one wall and above the refrigerator on another. Other cabinets stand next to the stove. We probably have more plywood cabinets in our kitchen than any household in East End. The door frames and the doors to the back porch and the dining room, the wainscoting, baseboards, and other wooden kitchen surfaces are painted with ivory-colored enamel.

The kitchen wallpaper is yellow. But what you recall about the kitchen is the plywood cabinets with the clear, reddish-brown stain on them to bring out their grain. I hardly remember the days Dad built them, but I know it took strength for him to work eight-hour shifts at the shipyard, then come home to care for the house—painting it, changing storm windows, cutting the grass outside—then to go down the basement to his cabinet project. I think he is the strongest man alive.

Here are four reasons for my thinking this: His gruff boss, who doesn't shave and can't pronounce Polish names, thinks Dad, because of our last name, likes to be called Car Wash. When the boss yells, "Car Wash, do this," "Car Wash, do that," Dad smiles. Everyone believes Dad's good-natured; but I think his smile means he's stronger than most for not losing his temper, which he has a right to lose considering he had a life-threatening accident in the shipyard where the boss makes fun of him. Self-possession is one of Dad's great strengths, and there are others. Example two, for instance—he labors all year in cold and snow, heat and pouring rain. Or example three—in addition to being called Car Wash and working in bad weather, he suffers another insult in silence: Across the highway from the Great Lakes freighter the men are lengthening in dry dock stands a Greyhound bus. Nothing else is there but the Greyhound, which a 1940s baseball team or band toured in—no buildings, no trees, just the broken-down bus with flat tires that someone parked in the field. On a piece of cardboard over the smashed front window, the owner has written, POLISH SKI TEAM.

Stanley "Car Wash" Karawinski says nothing about this. Nor, for my fourth example of his strength, did he say a word when I went with him on his bicycle to the Alibi Tavern and a drunk yelled, "Hey, Car Wash, you're Polack, right?" When Dad didn't respond, the guy said, "Well, a Polack's nothin' more than a sandblasted n—gger." Though I was only thirteen at the time, I thought about telling the drunken man to be careful who he was talking to, but Dad laughed and left with a bottle of brandy for Grandfather.

He looked shaken on the way home, his face set in the grim smile he's had since the accident. "He shouldn't call black people that or call us Polacks," he said.

When we parked his bike in the garage, he was bothered he hadn't answered the guy in the Alibi. Yet I know a strong man can have a peaceful heart. Violence would have done no good. Though he didn't stand up for himself, I knew my father had honor and integrity. No matter if people called us Polacks, he always cared enough about the country of our ancestors to fly the Polish flag in our yard. Today we also have a decal on our front window—over a red eagle the word SOLIDARNOŚĆ, Solidarity, in white letters; for in Poland this year, the Communist government raises food prices and dismisses workers from shipyards and coal mines and keeps Solidarity leaders in concentration camps. Dad cares about this because he is also Polish and works in a shipyard, where he pedals to work on Mother's old bicycle, a Schwinn with thick tires, a blue frame and fenders, and a white seat. In bad weather, Tony Stromko gives him a ride.

• • •

But I should describe the rest of our house. On the table in our dining room stands a statue of the Virgin Mary; under Her is a lace tablecloth. Thinking that the Blessed Virgin had Her favorite television programs, when I was young I used to turn Her statue toward the TV room next to the dining room. Now Grandfather, who has emphysema and needs his privacy, lives in that room. For the Mother of God there's not much to watch on TV anyway. Behind the crucifix on the dining room wall, my mother tucks the palm frond after Palm Sunday Mass; and in the

TV room are Dziaduś's bed, an end table with a lamp on it, and a commode, because it's hard for him to get to the bathroom during the night.

We call the last downstairs room the "front room." If you look in from the yard through the picture window, you'll see a piano, phonograph, sofa, desk (on it a framed picture of Dad as a young man when he was still okay before the accident), comfortable chairs, and a large wall mirror. If you look out the window, you'll see Washington Park stretch from Fourth to Fifth Street and from Twenty-fifth Avenue East to the railroad tracks that run to the Fredericka Flour Mill. This is the downstairs of a house of memory.

Because Dad can't talk much on the job, he keeps everything stored up 'til suppertime, when out come the most beautiful stories as well as fantastic tales that a soon-to-be Marquette freshman shouldn't believe, like the one about Mr. Novotny, who wore a hook on his arm after an industrial accident. How can you anticipate a story like this—that Mr. Novotny welded his hook to the bumper of a car? Yet Dad insists it happened. He says: "I heard him calling, 'Help! Someone help!' The poor, drunken Novotny is crying when he sees me. His shirt's greasy, his pants sliding down his hips. 'Get me loose, Car Wash,' he says. Giving a pull where 'Captain Hook' welded himself to the bumper, I broke him free." (The indentation in Dad's forehead from the accident grows shallower as he tells us the story.) "So he stands up, thanks me, stumbles out the garage door, reaches up with his hook to clamp himself to the clothes line he rigged from there to the house, and guides himself by the rope across the yard to the back porch."

"It's a safety line for drunks," Grandfather says.

By now Dziaduś and I don't know what is true or false; then Dad tells the story of how he was sailing on the Great Lakes ore carrier *Arthur M. Anderson* when the ship was inundated by migrating warblers that settled on the deck at dusk, awoke at dawn, then flew on their journey north. "Thing is," Dad told us, "they lost ground because we were going *southwest.*"

This is the mysterious "Car Wash" the storyteller—Stanley Karawinski, who stands six-feet-one-inch tall, shoulders slumped when he walks, who has a twist of brown hair partly covering his forehead and a ruddy face from working outside. He hears rumors and gossip and wants exciting things to happen to him, though how could he have been at Novotny's and at work at the same time? I give him the benefit of the doubt concerning the truth of his stories. On the other hand, why was he quiet in the Alibi Tavern or after Sunday Mass, when people stood out front of church? Mother does all the socializing there. I think Dad is "slow" from what happened to him when a gantry crane dropped a hull plate to the earth. Hitting the ground, it banged against a smaller crane and struck him. Then I reassure myself that because he rides a bike with a wicker basket tied to the handlebars, doesn't hurry his speech, and usually only talks at home doesn't mean anything bad. Figuring he's still capable of accomplishing big things in life, I apply a saying to him Dziaduś taught me: "*Krowa co dużo ryczy, mało mleka daje* . . . Great talkers are little doers." Outside of our home, Dad is no talker.

• • •

Last week while we were waiting for Dad to come home from work, Mother was preparing supper, Dziaduś was at the table, and I was in the pantry off of the kitchen, thinking back on high school, specifically how one teacher says reading Polish names is like reading an eye chart. After you heard it a thousand times—Polish names = eye chart—it wasn't funny. Right off in our freshman year, he shortened Zawistowski to "Zowie," Kiszewski to "Kazoo," "Waletzko" to "Waldo," which is like what happens to Dad's name at the shipyard. This is the same teacher who, if you wrote a confusing sentence on the board, called it a "Polish sentence" in front of everyone, no matter if you were Polish or not.

Trying to forget all that, I went to the kitchen table where Dziaduś read the Marine Vessel Traffic part of the newspaper to see which Polish ships were upbound from Sault Ste. Marie to the Port of Superior. Boats with names like *Ziemia Chelmińska, Pomorze Zachodnie, Zakopane,* and *Ziemia Białostocka* have put in here a hundred times to load grain and flax seed. Dziaduś was like the harbormaster of our house, the way he knew everything about the port. I couldn't get mad at him; for when he looked at me, it was like he was asking, "Why am I a widower? Why are my lungs failing? Why are my days at sea over? Why did my son get hurt in the shipyard?" When Dziaduś tapped his fingers on the tabletop, I got his watch or fetched his sweater from the armchair. "Can I do anything else for you, Grandfather?"

"It's hard to breathe in here. There's nothing anybody can do," he replied.

"I know. Is there a Polish boat in this week?"

"*Ziemia Gniezniéńska* at Harvest States Elevator," he might say. "Let's talk when there's more air."

"I'd like to talk about the boats with you," I told him.

Then I started thinking *why* about my own life. I was sick of hearing about how our names look like eye charts, of hearing about "Polish sentences." I even heard a radio disk jockey say, on the air, "Another frickin' Polack name," when he was announcing the winners of free concert tickets and he stumbled over a good name ending in *-czyk.* Why do people say such things when my father spent a year on a gunboat on a river in South Vietnam; when Dziaduś sailed waters patrolled by German U-boats during World War II; when ten Polish seamen have jumped ship in Superior to start a new life here; when on this very day coal miners, shipyard, and transit workers are fighting the Communists in Poland? How can someone joke about such strong men? Of all ethnic groups, the Polish seem to be the ones people get away with ridiculing.

Having put supper in the oven, Mother was in the front room listening to the phonograph, a polonaise by Chopin. She said it expressed Polish people's courage and spirit. The polonaise reminded me of her. So did a prelude called "The Revolutionary," which Chopin wrote in Paris to honor the 1831 Polish uprising against the Russians. A dreamlike nocturne reminded me of my father. I was too young to know much of what he was like before the accident, but I knew I admired him for what he'd been through.

Nocturne

Prelude

Polonaise

Once on the gym stage before a program the nuns sponsored, Sister Leokadia placed a bust of Chopin on a pedestal. I'd come to turn the pages of her music. After she finished practicing the piano, she told me to wait for her while she went to get something. When she returned, she gave me a yellow rose to place on the pedestal. The American and Polish flags stood on either side of the bust. "Go ahead, Stefa," she said. After I put the rose before the great composer (as I will present my father a rose some day when I show him my Marquette diploma), I touched the stars on the blue field of the American flag and held the red and white Polish flag. Kissing both flags, I heard Chopin's music in the still air. He is dear to the hearts of Polish people. In the national anthem of Poland, which begins "*Jeszcze Polska Nie Zgineła* . . . Oh, our Poland shall not perish, while we live to love her*," you hear the strains of a polonaise. Polish money has

Chopin's picture on it. A famous statue of him stands in Łazien-
ki Park in Warsaw.

· · ·

With summer passing, I was thinking, as Mother played
Chopin on the phonograph, how I'd miss the house, the nuns,
and my family when I went to college. Then the door opened
and the bicycle rider stepped in.

A stranger stood on the back porch. Looking like he was
thirty-five or forty, he wore a sailor's blue watch cap, his hair
sticking out from under it. A brown suit coat hung off his shoulders, the cuffs pinned under to shorten them. A cream-colored
shirt stood out from beneath the coat. As I was thinking how out
of place the man looked, Dad said, "*Gość w dom, Bóg w dom* . . . A
guest in the house is like God in the house."

"Who's this?" asked Mother. She was always patient with
Dad. Smelling cigarette smoke on his clothes, she knew he'd
been drinking somewhere.

"He's off a ship. We were in the Warsaw Tavern. There's an
article in the paper. 'Immigration mum on ship-jumper.'"

"That's the Polish boat *Ziemia Gńieznieńska* was in port,"
Dziaduś said.

When Dad grows excited, Mother has to calm him. "We
have a Polish sailor right here," he was saying proudly.

"Pleace, I am—," said the man. Leaning against the sink, he
looked sorrowful, beaten-down.

"No more beer, Stanley," Mother said to my dad, trying to
coax him into his usual routine of telling stories.

"Here's a story for tonight," Dad said. "Tell us what happened to you, Wiktor Urbaniak."

Unsure of his place in our midst, one minute the sailor tried
to stand up straight and smile at us. The next minute, his forehead would wrinkle, he'd look angry, his shoulders would slump.

"*Buk-ser,*" he said. "I am in America six days. If I stay until ship leaves, then Immigration Office not so much problem for me. There would be no way to go for me to Poland. When I left ship, I shouted 'Kommuneest' at the captain, crazy man yelling down from bow. Instead of taking taxi cab, I am ending up with long-shoreman who I am lucky was in his car watching. Now I am reported to Immigration and Naturalization. *Buk-ser, Buk-ser,*" he repeated.

Dad got a bottle of beer for himself and one for our visitor. "Ten sailors have jumped ship here in five years," Dad said. "All in Superior, and I've never seen one 'til now."

"No beer for either of you," Mother said. "And that sailor is already drunk."

"But I have to join him in Solidarity, Helen."

When Dad finished sipping his beer, he went into the dining room, returning with his camera and with articles he'd been saving about shipyard workers in Gdańsk. "I'm also a shipyard laborer," he told the sailor. "I've been keeping up with your history like we're one and the same. I've got a Solidarity sticker in the window."

The sailor signaled me to get him another beer. I was afraid not to. He had scars where his eyebrows joined the temples. He had a mark on his forehead. It was like his face had been smashed up.

Dad pointed to his own forehead, where you could see the effects of the accident. "See where I got hurt? Did the Secret Service do that to your face? Helen, take a picture of us."

"*Buk-ser,*" said the seaman.

"I had an accident," Dad said. "Hull plate missed killing me. I got banged up."

"If you want to stay in the U.S., you better not drink so much," Mother said to Wiktor Urbaniak. "You'll need to go to INS again."

"Helen, Stefa," Dad said, "you don't know what's happening in your own kitchen. This is history taking place with him here. They arrest people in Poland all the time. I have an interest in things as a shipyard laborer. I know they can't beat down our spirit."

"You don't know Solidarity from the dairy store," Mother said.

"Buk-ser," said the sailor.

"By golly, here, stand by the stove so people will know it's in our kitchen we took the picture," Dad said. "Make a *V* for Victory and smile. Here, hold this, too." It was an oven mitt that said *"Polska Kuchnia,"* which means "Polish kitchen."

Ringed by the stove, refrigerator, plywood cabinets, the sailor tucked his square jaw into his chest. He swung a fist as though trying to loosen up his arms and shoulders.

As Mother said, "I know what he's saying. He means he's been a boxer," Dad said, "Solidarity," and whistled the "Hymn to Solidarity" the Gdańsk workers rally around.

When Dad extended his hand to him, Wiktor Urbaniak's hand came back in a way Dad didn't expect. The sailor had had enough picture taking. When my father said *"buk-ser"* not yet realizing what the drunk sailor meant by the word, Wiktor Urbaniak put up his guard.

Dad blocked the punch the sailor threw. It was as though Mr. Urbaniak off the *Ziemia Ghieznieńska* was shadow boxing.

"What's he punching anything for?" asked Mother.

"To show his solidarity with me," Dad said.

Moving his head from side to side, the sailor looked between his fists, oven mitt on one hand. "Problem?" he said, pronouncing it *"Pdob-lem,"* as he threw another punch that missed.

When my father dropped his guard, saying, "Hold on a second; I said 'Solidarity,'" a fist connected. Dad's eye swelled. He got hit again. I heard the wind rush out of him as he muttered

"Poland." Trying to clear out what he'd just learned, my dad shook his head. Tasting his bloody lip with his tongue, he was saying, "There's been a mistake."

When Dad's smile returned, Mother, angry, said to the sailor, "He's not right. Can't you see? Why do you think his forehead's like that and he rides a bicycle everywhere? He's not been okay for fourteen years. His daughter is the only one who can't see that," she said, pointing to me. Then to the sailor, she said, "You're getting out. Come on. We don't want you here, Solidarity or not."

I didn't know where they took the sailor. As my dad washed his face trying to sober up, Mother and Dziaduś drove Wiktor Urbaniak back to the Warsaw Tavern or to the Immigration Office. I didn't care where, not while Dad sat at the kitchen table talking to himself, head in his hands. He couldn't figure what'd happened, but I knew that a drunken immigrant seeking asylum didn't care what "Car Wash" Karawinski thought about world affairs. They lived in different countries.

Seeing Dad bewildered, I wanted to do what Sister encouraged us to do in our lives. She'd say it over and over, "*Nigdy nie przegap okazji, żeby powiedzieć komuś ze go kochasz* . . . Never waste an opportunity to tell someone you love them." But I couldn't do that right now, not when he was so busy shaking his head as he tried to explain things to himself. He was talking in a whisper about Gdańsk, about the Alibi Tavern, the shipyard . . . everything that made him feel special.

When he said he was all right and wanted to be alone for awhile, I went out to the garage for his bike. With Grandfather and Mother still away and my dad resting, there was no one to talk to. The house and yard were quiet. A far-off train whistle made me lonely. What did all this mean? I wondered as I rode the bike across the lawn to the front sidewalk. By the time I turned toward St. Adalbert's grade school, it was dark. You could smell lilacs, and I was glad to be out of the house. There'd been drinking and rough talking in our Polish kitchen. Dad had been embarrassed he couldn't stick up for himself. I figured what happened would cure him of the need to talk after work. Earlier during the drunken chatter he told us that Alphonse Zukowski, a Polish man who ran the auto body repair shop on Winter Street, owned the Polish Ski Team bus. I guess Mr. Zukowski thought it was harmless for Polish people to laugh at themselves or to be laughed at by non-Polish people.

It made *me* laugh knowing Mr. Zukowski's joke was on us Poles. As I rode along, I thought someone like Mr. Zukowski wouldn't care for Chopin. And regarding my father, the joke was on *me*, on Stefanie—"Stefancha" if you pronounce it the Polish way. I never wanted to admit my dad was slow, that he was confused by things. Once I acknowledged it, I laughed all four blocks to Sister Leokadia. When I arrived, I wasn't laughing anymore, for *she* knew what was courageous and noble in a spirit like my father's. Sister Leokadia knew everything.

As I walked across the school lawn, I could hear through the open gym window Sister practicing a nocturne, my father's music. The nocturne was moving and sad—like Poland must be this night. As the music rose into the darkness, I wondered whether the great Chopin heard it in heaven, whether Dziaduś and Mother heard it, whether Stanley "Car Wash" Karawinski heard it at home in our Polish kitchen. A laborer confused by things people took for granted, my dad's only fault was he had to tell the stories most people didn't want to hear. In doing so, he thought he'd make himself into someone he wasn't. I hoped he'd forgive me for thinking this about him; but I am his daughter, Stefancha the storyteller, and maybe when accidents happen to me, a nocturne will express who I am, too.

Nocturne

Prelude

Polonaise

As I entered the St. Adalbert's gymnasium and saw Sister
with a rose for Chopin, I knew I'd remember how, to honor her,
fireflies came out for the first time that summer. I also knew that
during this evening, I'd tell Dad the saying Sister Leokadia had
taught us. "Never waste an opportunity to tell someone you love
them." I would bow to my father and tell him this in Polish.

The Bird That Sings in the Bamboo

THE ACCIDENT that earned Lance Corporal Thaddeus Milszewski the Purple Heart during his first tour of duty in Vietnam could have been avoided. Because Sergeant Farrazzi was in a hurry to feed the grunts in the field, chow hadn't been secured when the truck left DaNang. When the deuce-and-a-half veered sideways, twelve loaves of rye bread pummeled the lance corporal's head and a nine-pound ham broke two of his ribs. He'd nearly drowned in a sea of chipped beef when kitchen pots, washtubs, and field stoves fell on him in the bed of the truck.

After a second harrowing tour in Vietnam—he was now back in Superior, his service hitch over—he cried out during his long nights, "Where am I?"

His mother came rushing in. "You're home. Your war days are over, son. You were calling, 'Help! Help!' Go to sleep. You've got college classes tomorrow."

"I can't sleep."

What he called "post-romantic stress disorder" tormented him. As he lay awake, he recalled how a simple thing like stirring cream corn and baking hot hamburger dishes for the hungry troops had indirectly led to his present lovesick predicament. Instead of being stuck in the field with an artillery or an infantry company during his second tour, he'd been free, as a camp cook, to go to the beach a few miles away to swim, drink beer, toss a football, or relax and stare at the glistening sea—or at the young woman he *still* couldn't put out of his mind.

A peasant salesgirl, half-French, half-Vietnamese, she was sixteen. He dreamed of her beautiful, delicate face, her finely formed hands and wrists as early morning breezes rustled the elm trees outside his boyhood window. She'd worn a black silk shirt and pants when he first saw her; on her feet were flip-flops made of recycled tires.

"You buy?" she'd approached him that day as he headed to the truck that would take him back to his outfit. "For you and frien' back at camp."

In a tray hanging from the rope about her shoulders were cigarettes and chewing gum.

"I'm Thaddeus Milszewski of 'America's Dairyland' in the state of Wisconsin. Pronounce my name right, and I'll buy something from you," he'd said. "I've been here eight months. I'm on my second tour."

"Ta-doos," she'd said.

"It's 'Ta-*de*-oosh,'" he replied.

Then she told him her name—Khuyen Vo.

It sounded like "Quinn" or "Queen Vo" to him. He asked her to tell him the Vietnamese words for "beach," for "sand," for "water," for "jungle," for "the bird that sings in the bamboo." When he bought a pack of chewing gum and whistled to imitate the bird, she knew he meant *Son ca*. "Ve'namese farmer like that bird. Sing morning to nigh'. It called skylark bird," she said. "When I try to learn English, soldier tell me what bird's name is in America."

What could he imitate for her next—water lapping against the fishing junk offshore, red eyes painted on its bow to ward off evil spirits? He told her he'd return on the next clear day for more gum.

"Khuyen Vo here in afternoo'," she said. "Mother have shop where you ca' find me. She sells many things, but I carry only a little tray."

"I gotta go. We're allowed five hours here," he said, imitating the bird's song as he waved to her from up the beach.

That night with the guys talking and playing cards, he rearranged his belongings in a seabag, wrote a letter to his parents. Later, in his cot beneath the mosquito net, he thought of Khuyen Vo. At 0100 hours, 1 A.M., he imitated the skylark beneath his breath. The next morning when he stopped for a drink of water from the lister bag, he imitated the skylark, softly, and the morning after as he prepared French toast for the troops.

• • •

In two weeks, he returned to China Beach. At the shops built of flattened cans and scrap wood, marines hung around drinking beer, Vietnamese rum, Coca-Cola. "Tiger"-brand cigarettes cost ten piasters a pack. But where was Khuyen Vo? He'd learned during his first tour not to pin his hopes on anything good happening in this godforsaken place. Still, when a voice said, "No buy cigarette?" he was afraid to turn around for fear it wasn't her.

"I never smoke, but I'll buy some gum," he said.

"What's my name?" she asked, smiling beneath the shade of her straw *nón lá* as she straightened it. She adjusted the rope on her shoulders that supported the tray.

"Queen," he said. "Here, let's split a stick of Doublemint. Sit down. How are you? I haven't been here for a few weeks. I couldn't get away."

"I no stop work ri' now. Have to earn money."

"Just rest here," he said.

"I sit five minute, rest. Practice English."

The colored gum wrappers reminded him of the counter Mrs. Odgorski tended by the cash register in the East End drugstore back home. "Double your pleasure, double your fun," he said, unwrapping a stick of gum for her.

"I no often meet soldier like you," she said. "Only hear soldier gun shooting far away at night."

"They're firefights," said the lance corporal. "I'll protect you."

"How you protec'? You have sore leg. Can't go far. I watch you walk. You long time in Ve'nam? Have girlfriend? Why you sad when you talk to me?" she asked, savoring the taste of the gum.

"I was in an accident on my last tour here. No, I'm sure not sad, and no one's waiting for me at home. Do you have a boyfriend?"

"Khuyen Vo no have time for boyfrien' 'til she twenty-five. I someday go to Saigon Medical School. In two year' I want to take first 'concourse' exam to be a doctor. I go to school mornings."

When she smiled, he saw how white her teeth were. She'd reddened her lips with lipstick. It looked as though she'd brushed them against a tropical flower. Her white teeth, olive-colored skin, black hair and eyebrows under the *nón lá*—he couldn't stop looking at her. The two of them sampled a piece of Spearmint next. "I promised I'd be here," he said. "How do you like this flavor?"

"Khuyen Vo like it because you buy from her," she said.

"In America you chew a flavor until you tire of it, then you switch. It's the same with many things," he said. "Your tray is like at the drugstore in the neighborhood where I live—except there you have twenty-five brands of cigarettes plus pipe tobacco plus cigars. Mrs. Odgorski sees that they're fresh, or Art Haugen would get mad. He's the owner, but she's in charge of the greeting cards, newspapers, magazines, confections."

"I don't know what are those things," said Khuyen Vo.

"They're nice to have if you like variety."

"Ve'namese cannot double their pleasure very easy. That's why I want to go to Saigon, study. Then I help people. I study in school to learn English and science."

"So you have no boyfriend?"

"No interest. I tol' you I study and have no time. You don't listen."

She was right about him not listening.

• • •

After two more weeks, she was out of chewing gum. In the United States, twenty packs cost a dollar. Here he'd spent six dollars for twenty-one packs of gum. In addition to his pay, he was receiving an overseas allotment plus hazardous duty pay. What did he care what he spent?

"I like Black Jack, Dentyne, Beaman's Clove. There's a dance on TV advertising this one gum, Teaberry. You start with your legs together, then move them apart," he said. "The music for 'The Teaberry Shuffle' goes 'Ta-dadada-dada.' You skip your feet a little, scissor your legs fast, go back to— I look stupid imitating it for you, don't I? There's a railroad trestle by our house you get to by cutting through the woods where the smell in fall reminds you of Juicy Fruit. Aspen trees smell like that. Shutting my eyes, touching the cellophane on these cigarette packs, I can recall home like I'm there at the drugstore counter or fiddling with my buddy's pack of cigarettes. The car's running, I'm turning the radio dial, he's getting our food orders at the Frostop Drive-In. A lot of stuff brings you home in your mind so you're not in the war."

"Maybe in Saigon I will feel that way," Khuyen Vo said. "It far from family here. South Ve'nam government pay for the university and medical school. However, I must pass concourse examination to stay. When I leave here in two year, life is different for me in Saigon."

"I remember when I left home this last time. Man, I got drunk, worried, switched my thinking a hundred times about coming back to Vietnam, but now I'm happy I signed up for a second tour."

• • •

She returned one day with a red flower from a *Phùòng* tree in town. As he practiced saying the name, she told him it symbolized the end of school, since it always blooms in May. "To student who has vacation from school but will be separated from friend and teacher, the bloom of the *hoa Phùòng* represents sadness as well as happiness," she said. She was lucky to find the flowers so fresh, because during the rainy season they fall from the tree.

In return for the flower, the lance corporal gave her a map. They unfolded it on a table behind her mother's shop. Khuyen Vo's mother didn't know whether to laugh or cry when she saw the marine with her daughter. After introducing the lance corporal to *ma mére,* Khuyen Vo excused herself to listen to the American say, "This is the railroad trestle I told you about. These cross-hatched lines are like a symbol for it."

"What this?"

"Neighborhood school, not mine though. The river is the Nemadji. It means 'Left-Handed River.' When Indians and French fur trappers came off Lake Superior, they saw the river on the left."

"French people like in Ve'nam? They look like me?" she asked.

"Yes, French. They named places Bois Brule, Au Sable, Isle Royale."

The topographical map showed low spots and elevations of hills, bays, rivers, creeks. Dots represented houses. Before he'd left home, he circled his own house in red. Parallel lines, a shovel, flags, and crosses indicated railroad tracks, a sandpit on Wisconsin Point, schools, churches. The long edge of the lake was blue.

They spent twenty minutes looking at the map. He handed her a stick of Juicy Fruit to give her an idea of the scent of his country in the fall. "Here's my grade school. These are neighborhood houses," he said. "There's St. Francis Church. It and mine, St. Adalbert's Church, are marked by a cross on top of the black square. I know it's hard to follow, but this is East Fourth Street. I walk it a lot going to and from the East End business district. Khuyen Vo, this is beside the point, but at the Superior Theater when I was in high school, there were talent contests. After the movie Friday night, local people like Mr. Buck Mrozek, who played 'The East End Polka' on the accordion, all competed. There were great bands playing then, too. The winner was to appear on *Jack Paar,* this famous TV show. Besides Buck Mrozek, now that I think of it, a few other old people had talent acts, but nobody except a band like Chet Orr and the Rumbles had a chance, because us teenagers always cheered for them. Week after week the competition went on. Just as the excitement peaked, the guy sponsoring the shebang took off. The police found out there'd been no arrangement made for anyone to be on *Jack Paar.*"

"Where did he go?"

"Skipped town. Someday I could take you to the showhouse. I'd buy you a malt at the drugstore. We'd eat hamburgers at the Arrow Café."

"I want to attend medical school."

"Why not study in the U.S.? There's a hospital halfway between St. Adalbert's and my house. See it here where I was born? Maybe you could be a doctor in this hospital."

To help her daydream about the United States and about how near his parents' red-circled house stood to the river, she asked to keep the map.

"If you'd like to have it, that'd be great," he said. He told her Wisconsin got cold in winter. When the river froze, people skated on it. "One time my grandpa caught a sucker through the ice that was record size and written about in our newspaper."

"The Mekong is only river here with giant fish that can be ten feet long. I sometimes eat *pla bük*. Maybe you cook for me?"

"I do enough cooking at the mess tent," the lance corporal said.

"Then you cannot expect Khuyen Vo to cure you when you need a doctor," she said, teasing him.

Her wanting the map . . . the lance corporal's cornering the chewing gum market; how could this hurt anyone when he had five months left in Vietnam? When she brought more red flowers, he gave her a miniature magnifying glass so she could read the topography of his home more easily. During the rainy season, she turned seventeen.

A few days later she guided his hands to her face. She listened to his heartbeat. They met almost every day through the end of September. One day that month, as she taught him to shape the red flower into a butterfly, he kissed her eyes when she closed them, and the butterfly flower dropped to the earth. Another time, when they were alone in the palms and banana plants behind her mother's shop, with only the sound of the bird in the bamboo, she told him that Saigon was four hundred and fifty miles through the highlands if she could travel the French

Colonial highway. After she explained how she'd take another route because the old highway was dangerous, Khuyen Vo returned the lance corporal's kiss.

• • •

From these matters of butterfly flowers and interludes among the banana plants, Khuyen Vo's love grew for the lance corporal, and she remained happy and trusting. The lance corporal, however, suspected that in his own case either the East End winters or Vietnam's rainy weather had done something terrible to his heart.

It was the first of October. Coincidental with one of their afternoons together, an opportunity came for him to return to the States early. Three hours after the lance corporal had told Khuyen Vo he'd never leave her, Thaddeus's gunnery sergeant decided to delay his own rotation to the United States until later in winter. That way he could take his wife to the St. Paul Winter Carnival. Then he would settle in to await a beautiful spring in Quantico, Virginia, his next duty station. Fond of the lance corporal, especially of the way he prepared a Polish meal, the gunny said, "You take my rotation day, Milszewski. You have as much time in Vietnam as I do this tour. I'll give you an earlier travel slot. How's the beginning of January? I'll cut your orders if you want out of here. A good cook deserves the gratitude of his nation."

How often the lance corporal dreamed of home. Though it would be twelve below zero and snow would be piled high on the roadsides, he'd be in Superior much sooner than planned if he accepted the gunny's offer. Considering the possibilities life now presented, he'd propose marriage to Khuyen Vo the next time he saw her, and later, on China Beach, they'd figure out the details of their life together. If he wanted to rotate ahead of time, he'd still have a few months with her before having to make up his mind.

As they walked up the beach the next afternoon, he thought,
Why worry her now? Why tell her I might leave? The day was
too beautiful for anything so serious. She made him stay in the
dune grass while she walked to the shore. "What are you doing?"
he called to her.

"I show you where *I* live," she said.

With a stalk of sea grass, she drew lines in the elevation in
the sand near where he sat. Where the slope in the sand was
sharper, her contour lines ran closer together. On a topographical map, intervals between lines mean a ten-foot rise. After plot-
ting the land, she drew an outline of his fingers, writing beside
the outline the words she was whispering as she ran her other
hand over the scar on his leg. She brought her face to his neck,
lay against him so that they could watch the forest beyond the
dunes.

He kissed her. (Why tell her anything right now? Why not
surprise her once the gunny's news sank in? He could return
home, go to college, send for her.) When he put his hands
beneath her silk shirt and kissed her, she kissed him, too. When
he told her he'd never leave someone so beautiful and that one
day they'd be married, he wondered why she looked sad. "I
won't ever leave you, you know that," he said. They lay in the
sun, protected from the sea breeze by the dunes. He told her
there were places like this where he lived. He pretended now
that they were in northern Wisconsin and she was going to meet
his parents.

"Will your family be on the beach of Lake Superior?" she
asked, going along with his game.

"Yes, that's their driftwood fire down closer to the light-
house."

"Will they like to meet Khuyen Vo?"

"They know you from my letters."

"Will you be happy?"

"Sure. I'll take you all over town. Dad's a regular fellow. When you see it, you'll like my room at home. My sister had polio when we were kids, but she had an operation. She's okay. Ma's nice. My best friends are Bob Harnisch and Norm Lier. I have plenty of friends. Wait'll you see the neighborhood—" He couldn't stop talking.

"So they like me?"

"Yes," he said, sad to pretend, but not wanting to betray any more than he had to about his plans. It was best not thinking about anything but who might see them when they wanted to be alone. "Wait," he said as she undid the front of her black silk shirt. Certain no one was in sight, he reached for her and helped her off with her clothes.

• • •

"You're not sure you want to go home, are you, Milszewski? I don't want to force it on you," Gunnery Sergeant Fiandt said one day. "You got a girlfriend, I hear. Don't even think about bringing her Stateside. It'll never happen. Do you think our government gives a shit every time a twenty-year-old Polack jarhead with blue balls thinks he's in love? Shit, the red tape involved in such a marriage would drive a person buggy. Nobody's *that* much in love anyway to bring a gook to the land of the brave and the free! If you passed all the paperwork through on our side, which you probably would never get done, then you'd still have the South Vietnamese government fucking you over. They surely will, Ski, if you try to get her out of the country. Just as ARVN soldiers ain't worth a shit, neither is their government."

"I might leave her here for awhile, Gunny. I'm not sure. I know it's a lot of red tape to get her out of Vietnam, but I've got to try," the lance corporal replied. "I'm looking forward to a good, long rest in Superior, where I can think things out and decide."

"You deserve a rest," said the gunny. "Get your head screwed on, Ski. You don't need something like this mucking up your life. You don't want a slant-eye who prob'ly can't talk English walkin' down the aisle on your wedding day. No, do as your gunny advises. Keep your other head in your pants, and you'll be fine. Pray or something when you're together with her. It's only a temporary urge you feel for her. Hell, Ski, go to Dog Patch if you need to get laid so bad. You'll get your ashes hauled for three-hundred piasters and not have the red tape to worry about afterwards."

"I'll think about Dog Patch, Gunny, and about everything you say. I know things work against a person in life sometimes, so it's good to think things through."

"That's the ticket, Ski, to have plans."

Still, there was this girl. At 2 A.M.—0200 hours—listening to small-arms fire far away, he knew what his options were: either stay in Vietnam or go back home and find someone new in the States. Fifteen times he began letters home. "I'm staying here. I found somebody I love," he'd write his parents. Then he decided he'd return to Wisconsin and tell his congressman that she need-ed medical assistance, that they were married, that the govern-ment had an obligation to him, Tad Milszewski, citizen, veteran, to get her out of Vietnam. He told himself so many things he tired of thinking about them.

Then it was 5 A.M. Worn out with indecision and lack of sleep, he stacked eggs beside the stove and tinkered with the knob on the toaster.

• • •

When the sea grew roiled and clouds shrouded the Anna-mites, he gave her a Marine Corps ring he'd bought at the PX in

DaNang. "Wear it on a string around your neck, Khuyen Vo. We're engaged," he said. He gave her his old transistor radio. She was pleased with the thoughtfulness of a marine who, though she didn't know it, had gotten himself into something very deep. *Nobody* spent three tours in Vietnam! If he signed on for another one, his buddies in the outfit and people back home would think he was crazy. When he gave her the ring, he placed his hand on the map in a kind of pledge to her. "Remember, you're visiting home when you look at the map. You won't want to leave East End," he told her. They whispered their love to each other that day for so long he had to run to catch the liberty truck.

That evening she held the map and the ring and tried to play the transistor, but her lover had forgotten to change the batteries. Flushed with the excitement of their lovemaking, the lance corporal didn't think about rotating until the hour before midnight.

An eagle, globe, and anchor decorated the gilded sides of the ring. The clerk at the PX had told him the smooth red stone in the center was a garnet, the birthstone for January. After a week, Khuyen Vo was wearing the ring on her finger.

"Here's a photograph of our house," he told her when they met again in early January. "My parents' room is upstairs. It's behind these two windows. My room and my sister Anna's room are upstairs on the opposite side of the house. We can see Lake Superior from most every room in the house. You can keep the snapshot. To have a picture of the house will add to the meaning of the map for you."

"What room is ours?" asked Khuyen Vo.

"I guess my room will be ours. I'll get a job at the Water and Light as the night janitor. I know I can do it. We'll stay with my folks for a few months. Eventually, we'll need our own place. An apartment at the Euclid Hotel should be nice."

To steel himself as he described their future, he pulled out a newspaper movie ad from his wallet. He'd kept the ad since he left home. It read, "HUD—'The Man with the Barbed-Wire Soul.'" "Best movie ever," he told Khuyen Vo. Though the lance corporal didn't have a barbed-wire soul, he felt like he did as he tried to think how he could reconcile his desire for Khuyen Vo with the gunny's advice. Maybe the best thing would be to think of Paul Newman in *Hud*. Hud had women around, but he stayed cool. He never fell for them.

Khuyen Vo was so beautiful. "Do you love me, Ta-doos?" she asked him.

"I love you more than anyone. I'll take care of you," he said.

As they walked along the contoured shore, she asked what it meant to have a soul of barbed wire.

"It's a way of saying you have no feelings. When I close my eyes—I have to shut them real tight and clear my mind—then I have no feelings."

"You stay here with me?"

"I will. I was thinking if I ever went Stateside, it'd be only until I could make some plans for us."

"You're not going. Now is January. You stay, Ta-doos, 'til May and June like you tol' me?" she said, sensing his indecision.

"I'm not leaving," he said. "We're getting married in spring, I guarantee. But I might have to go home to prepare things for us."

Hearing this, she started crying, though the lance corporal couldn't understand why, since he felt good about the future. She wouldn't stop crying until he reassured her. As he did, he tried to clear his mind to get back to what the gunny said.

"Why your eyes closed, Ta-doos?" she asked.

• • •

In Vietnam, roads of red laterite soil become greasy mud in the rain, a few pieces of fish mixed with rice and some greens provide a family three or four satisfying meals, and Khuyen Vo's mother chews betel nut, which contains a mild narcotic, to numb the pain in her gums.

The lance corporal remembered all this a week later as the C-130 flew over China Beach to Kadena Air Force Base, in Okinawa. From there, he flew fourteen hours more to El Toro Marine Corps Air Station, in California, for debriefing and discharge. Two days later, he flew on Western Airlines to Minneapolis, then on Republic Airlines one and a half hours to Duluth.

In Superior, the lance corporal, who'd taken the gunny's advice and not said good-bye to Khuyen Vo, slept away the mornings in his parents' house. Why get worked up? He'd have had to rotate sooner or later, he told himself. For an enlisted man to bring a Vietnamese woman to America was nearly impossible; the gunny's words were ringing in his ears.

But by napping during the day, he couldn't sleep at night. Sometimes he remembered who had the topographic map. When his heart raced and there was no one but himself to listen to it, he thought of the bird that sings in the bamboo. In his boyhood bedroom, the one Khuyen Vo couldn't see in the picture, he thought of her and heard crows squawking outside, chiding him for being like Hud. In an effort to free his soul from the coil of wire, he went to confession. "I did something to a woman," he told the priest on the Feast of St. Blaise, in February. When Father Nowak, who disliked the war, asked, "What, Thaddeus?" the penitent said he'd fooled a woman into thinking they were getting married. "It was the only way to keep myself sane," Thaddeus said. "You'll have to make it right with her," said the priest. But when Father Nowak asked where the woman lived, and Thaddeus, seeking absolution in a confessional booth in the East End, told him, "Da Nang, South Vietnam," the priest realized all was hopeless. "There's no penance I can give you for that," he said and closed the confessional screen on Thaddeus.

Perhaps it was on the afternoon of this confession that the delicate Khuyen Vo believed her marine would bring her more engagement presents. She twisted the garnet ring from side to side, trying to read her future in the red stone. When February passed and the American with his wedding plans didn't show up, she sang the mournful song of a woman who waits for her lover by the Perfumed River. Her mother hummed along. In the shop hung a picture of a bridge beside which *Phượng* trees bloomed. "Someday flowers will bloom in our houses," she told her mother, sighing as she watched the rain make the roads impassable. In Vietnamese, she whispered to herself, "I am waiting a long, long time." When the rain stopped, she replotted the distance from the sea to the dunes. "Ta-doos," she said, drew lines in the sand with her fingers, then repeated the name, "Ta-doos."

By May, when certain red flowers almost the color of garnet bloom on trees in the schoolyards and along the banks of the DaNang River, Khuyen Vo, still pining for Thaddeus Milszewski, gave the American's map to an ARVN soldier, who hung it in a jungle post hidden behind a fortress of orchids. In a few months, the Viet Cong overran the post, as they would eventually overrun the country. Puzzling over the intelligence value of the map, the VC looked for hours at the "NE/4 Superior 15′ Quadrangle of Superior, Wisconsin." Especially disconcerting to them was a red-circled dot. What did it mean to their war effort, Milszewski's house by the river in Superior?

Meanwhile, the lance corporal was beginning to feel like his old self. He attended Mass, looked up friends. He could hardly believe he'd thought of staying in Vietnam in the first place. He was happily working part-time at the Water and Light. The autumn turned out to be as beautiful as anyone remembered. The yellowing aspen trees, the reddening maples brought out the leaf watchers in record numbers. Late into September, newspapers ran front-page photographs of the brilliant foliage along the Left-Handed River. Even in mid-October, Thaddeus Milszewski could see from his window driftwood fires up and down the Lake Superior shore.

He had enrolled in the state teacher's college in Superior. He was progressing very well in school, especially in geology class. While the younger students complained of having to memorize the texture of minerals, he learned, to his pleasure, that the geology course was also concerned with beaches and with the reading of maps. When these topics came up in early winter, he was ahead of his classmates, for he knew topography and felt his barbed wire soul to be completely healed from the maps of the past. But now he learned something new about map reading: that you could place aerial photographs side by side, then view them from a few inches above through magnified lenses. "Stereoscopic viewing" makes the subject of the photos appear three-dimensional. When he discovered that virtually all the world's beaches have been photographed, he put his heart to a test to determine whether it was healed.

One afternoon in geology class, he failed the test when he observed China Beach made so realistic that his tears blurred the stereoscope's lenses, and he spoke out with sudden passion about the action of waves upon a beach. "The tide shaped us. It shaped everything the whole time I was with her," he told his classmates, though who in a Wisconsin State College classroom could know what he was talking about? Startled to hear him, they looked around, rolled their eyes. As they started whispering, then snickering about his outburst, calling him "the lover" and "the war hero," the former lance corporal went back to his stereoscopic lenses. "There was nothing we could do. I can't leave her there," he was saying, though now he kept it more to himself.

President of the Past

YOU MAY JOIN our Polish Club if you are "an upright descendant of the Slavic race." If you are older than forty-five but of Slavic heritage, you must settle for "social membership status," in which case you can't hold office, vote on lodge matters, or receive sickness or death benefits; however, our by-laws state that social members can attend "all social doings on the society level." Our one social doing is a semiannual lunch of cabbage rolls, sausage, dark bread, and beer. In the late 1940s and throughout the 1950s when I accompanied my father, "Buck" Mrozek, to the club, things were different. The lodge hosted casino nights, dances, dinners, picnics. The bar was full even with no special events scheduled.

The son of the accordion player Buck Mrozek, I joined the club in middle age. After living in the Buffalo suburbs, the prospect of better employment drew me back. I paid the six-dollar membership fee and the twenty-two-dollar year's dues and was sworn in at Superior's Polish Club. A few years later, with no one willing to take over, I became president. At monthly meetings, I gain a sense of connectedness to something remembered and missed from the men who keep me in office.

One evening in the bar I heard how Joseph Smiegel rode a white horse in city parades years before. At home I have a photograph of him in uniform with the Gwardyo Pułaskiego ... the Pulaski Guard—a ceremonial military society founded in 1902. On leather helmets, *rogatywka,* an eagle rises above polished visors. Rising from the crown of the helmet, a pike holds a square leather top, from which feathered plumes fall to tunic collars. Epaulets decorate the men's shoulders, and braids run across the coat fronts. With sword drawn, Kapitan Smiegel stands before his men. Our display case holds his helmet and sash.

In the case in a corner of the bar also lies a medallion attached to a long, red ribbon. Printed on the medallion is CZŁONEK, "member," and on the ribbon with the delicately spun-gold border: TOWARZYSTWO ŚŚ PIOTRA I PAWŁA 1903, meaning "Society of Saints Peter and Paul 1903." Beside it hangs a black and silver ribbon that gives the date and place that the lodge was founded:

TOWARZYSTWO
Tadeusz Kościuszko
Zal. Dnia 1-go Sierpnia
1928 ROKU
W SUPERIOR, WISCONSIN

To go with this, we have a photo of an old wooden church. Mourners surround a casket whose half-open lid exposes the head and shoulders of a deceased man. Two lines of pallbearers and mourners in long winter coats and wearing Kosciuszko ribbons extend to the foreground in the photo: bare trees, snow, everyone staring at the photographer except the dead man, a lodge member who, at the center of the occasion in his honor, is left out. I don't recognize the living or the dead, but know them to be former lodge members by the ribbons on their coats and know they must not be forgotten.

Now when I pound the gavel and say, "The monthly meeting of the Thaddeus Kosciuszko Lodge is called to order," I look out at twenty or fewer ribbonless lodge brothers sitting on ragged chairs in a room above a bar. Fifty years ago there would have been four times that many members present. We hear an opening prayer, minutes of the previous meeting, the "Report of the Guardian of the Sick," and other agenda items before a closing prayer read by Frank Stepan, the vice president. Alone in the room after the members have gone downstairs for a beer, I try to remember what has gone on.

I will probably be the last president of the Polish lodge. The history of presidents will go from the son of an accordion player and a violin player (my mother performed for Calvin Coolidge when he had his "Summer White House" in Superior), all the way back to the men in the black coats in the funeral picture . . . back even to Kapitan Smiegel on the white horse.

This may happen very soon. The twenty-two thousand dollars in debts trouble us. Though the sign outside reads PUBLIC WELCOME, few nonmembers drop by to sit in the bar. The Polish national anthem has been replaced on the jukebox by a Frank Sinatra song. On some days, no one at all stops in at our club.

Two businessmen would like to turn it into an "interactive sports bar." A Finn and a German, they promise that if we sell to them and if the room upstairs isn't reserved, we can use it for monthly meetings and we can have a storage closet. But what about the *rogatywka*, sword, and sash in the glass case downstairs in the bar, or Mr. Gapa's 1914 account book in the office, showing whom he loaned money to so they could bring relatives here from the Old Country? These things would have to go into storage. With our past stored away, the club could disappear like Superior's Polish and Slovak churches. Churches gone, lodge membership dwindling, old people gone. If it keeps up, we'll have no memories. They'll all be in storage.

In the 1950s, when the club was in a building a few blocks
away, when the grain mills and "the World's Largest Ore Docks"
on Superior's waterfront were enjoying their best shipping seasons, and when, all in all, the world was a little younger, church,
Polish Club, and neighborhood were more important to people.
My father played the accordion. I hear him in memory. Within
earshot of his polkas in the East End lived my paternal grandparents, Antoni and Mary Mrozek, my aunts Ann Novack and
Cecilia Simzek, and my two great aunts who, never married,
took care of my great-grandfather Andrzej, who played obereks
on the concertina.

One day my daydreaming mother, who was done practicing
the violin, taught me about our history. My sister was out somewhere; my father was working at the flour mill. Just Mother and
I sat in a sunlit kitchen, a vase of lilacs between us.

"I want to tell you about the Black Madonna, Our Lady of
Częstochowa," she said. As she put down the violin, she stared
out the window at the warm May morning. "Centuries ago the
Swedes invaded Poland."

"What happened then?"

"They almost conquered Poland, except for this monastery
at Jasna Góra, where the Swedes saw a beautiful picture and
attempted to pull it from the wall. But the Madonna's picture
wouldn't budge. When a soldier cut Her face, others looked up
to see the Blessed Madonna bleed from Her wound. Seeing this,
the men fell to their knees, then fled. Then all the invaders withdrew, and Poland was saved."

That morning I wondered whether my mother missed her
own mother, who'd told her the legend of the Madonna. Perhaps
it was my mother's violin playing that made her recall the story
for me. Grandmother Rowinski, my maternal grandmother,
lived one and a half miles away in another part of the East End.

We didn't see her quite as often as other relatives who lived closer, because my father worked long hours, and my mother couldn't drive a car and was busy with my sister and me. Mother could dream, however.

On the day she told me about the Black Madonna, I think she missed her mother and the Old Country. My mother had been playing "Dreamer's Waltz . . . *O Młynarce z Pewnej Wsi Walc.*" In fact, my mother's side of the family was more the dreamers, the romantics, it seemed to me; my father's side was more practical. Was this the year the apple tree showered and blessed us with its blossoms one Sunday after Mass when Mother set a table outside for breakfast? Our peonies bloomed around the time the apple tree did. Pink apple blossoms would be clinging to the wire stand supporting the peonies. Soon delicate white lilacs would come out, then orange poppies. She'd daydream as she did on the morning of my history lesson, then play the violin with orange flowers for her backdrop. The way she told me the legend of Our Lady seemed like a dream—a personal, maternal introduction of a son to ancestral custom. I thank her for this. And during this time in the evening after work, Buck Mrozek, composer of the famous "East End Polka" and my father, practiced his accordion, so he, too, could dream. I bless and thank both parents for their lessons.

• • •

Now I think of the club and of my family as I whisper prayers. I don't want to let the club go to a German and a Finn, because the few active members who remain know our ancestors met during these very same summer and winter hours as we do, read the same opening prayer at meetings, and followed the same order of business: the "Report on Members Whose Suspensions Have Been Lifted," the "Report of the Guardian of the Sick . . ." The Polish and American flags stood before them as they do before us. How can we let this go? How can I myself let the club go? Almost everything is in storage. Yet in the faded map of Poland on the wall, in the display case, in the flag that needs washing, and in the stale air of the Polish Club, I still have a place to come to where I can cherish my heritage.

When Mr. Kubos, our sergeant-at-arms, isn't well and I, president, have to prepare the upstairs room for the meeting, I don't say much, realizing it is a job I must do. I live in a Pulaski Room of memories and write them over and over as though I were practicing a musical instrument, say, a violin that is playing "Dream Waltz" or an accordion playing "East End Polka." When during the course of a lodge meeting, I ask, "Are there any new members?" no one says anything in the Pulaski Room. No one joins the society. I myself don't talk much afterward either, just have a beer to forget where we are heading. I don't want to leave the hall. I don't want the hall's memories to go. I'm afraid of what will happen when they do. I, Rick Mrozek, am president of the past.

· · ·

When you walk outside after a meeting, after the closing prayer and the beer, when you walk out and the same gray, winter sky meets you that met other worthy lodge brothers for over seventy years . . . that met Smiegel and the Guard, you see a block south of here one of Superior's passenger train depots, closed now. Look the opposite way north two blocks into the hard wind stinging your eyes and whipping the Polish flag, and you see where the first club stood that meant so much to others and to me when I went there as a child with my father. There is a story about the closing of the old, rickety building. When the pounding feet of polka dancers weakened the foundation, the fire marshal said he'd have to close the Polish Club because the foundation was giving way under the heavy pounding of the feet. How could you make dancers stop when the air was blue with smoke or when the beer flowed or when the accordion player, fingering his keys, promised "Pennsylvania Polka" or my father's "East End Polka"?

When the building *was* condemned (too much dancing finally), the Thaddeus Kosciuszko Lodge, the Polish Club, bought the new hall, where I am president. This was so long ago: 1963. Here at the new clubrooms, the membership thought there'd be no problems with "sympathetic vibrations," the engineering term for what occurred at the old club. The new brick building with the flags out front looks like a pillbox. The bar portion lies below ground. Diesels shunting boxcars in the nearby freight yards couldn't shake these walls. Two dozen accordion-playing lodge members, my father among them, couldn't shake unshakable walls.

If, after the meetings in the unshakable building these days, feeling slightly shaken you drive past the shipyards, you still see ore boats laid up for winter repairs. At the elevators, grain still rots in wet, stinking piles. Along Belknap Street, if you go home that way toward East End, the storefronts are run-down as they were in 1928. Little has been done to beautify Superior since Kapitan Smiegel appeared on a white horse.

Years ago my uncles Augie and Louie, my mother's brothers, would have returned from lodge meetings this way, down Belknap to their parents', my maternal grandparents', house. My maternal grandfather, Wincenty Rowinski, would have come home this way, too. His dreaming grandson, I, Rick Mrozek, drive home past their house on the way to my own. Now I wonder where I have come to at age fifty-eight, into what strange dream of old neighborhoods, where no relatives live anymore.

My dreaming grandmother, who left Poland when she was fourteen—and whom my dreaming mother missed so terribly that she played the violin to think of her—and my grandfather Wincenty built their East End home near the Northern Pacific railroad tracks. Grandmother would have heard trains passing north, then west to Duluth, and passenger trains heading east to Ashland, Wisconsin, or to Ewen and Marquette, Michigan. I wonder whether eighty years ago with my grandfather at the flour mill, Grandmother, alone in her kitchen with the sprig from the lilac bush in her hand, ever whispered to the passing trains, "Where have I come to?" as she looked out at the empty fields and at the trains that might bring Polish people to Superior. Quiet and gentle like my mother, she spoke little in either language except when she was dreaming.

Now I try to speak her language, the old people's language, when I say, "Babusia, are you there in the kitchen window? It is eighty years ago. Is Grandfather Wincenty gone to work at the flour mill? Is Mother at a violin lesson? Is the Black Madonna's picture hanging on the wall?" In my grandmother's back yard, if I could again go there as a child, I would pass the rain barrel beside the barn, pass Augie's garden, pass Louie's goldfish pond, where the gladioli were cleared back beneath the apple tree. That's where I'd look for my maternal grandmother, the dreamer with her lilac sprig. This is the place I'd look for memories of all my ancestors. Maybe now—having seen parents and grandparents die in the East End and my great-aunts Helcha and Fronia and uncles Władziu, Louie, and Augie die—maybe now at my age and as president of a Polish lodge that is declining, I could get from them the answers I seek to make this remembering easier.

I am a president of the past, calling the meeting of ghosts to order.

ANTHONY BUKOSKI grew up in the Polish East End neighborhood of Superior, Wisconsin. A year after graduating from high school, he enlisted and served as a Marine in South Vietnam. Upon his discharge from the service, he finished his B.A. with a double major in English and German at the University of Wisconsin-Superior. He received an M.A. in English from Brown University, an M.F.A. in creative writing from the Iowa Writers' Workshop, and later a Ph.D. in English from the University of Iowa. He now teaches English at his alma mater in the port city where his Polish emigré grandparents first settled. His stories have been nominated four times for the Pushcart Prize, have twice won special mention, and have appeared in many literary venues in the U.S. and Canada including *New Letters, Quarterly West,* and *The Literary Review.* He is the author of three other story collections, *Twelve Below Zero* (1986), *Children of Strangers* (SMU, 1993), and *Polonaise* (SMU, 1999). He is currently at work on a novel. He and his wife Elaine live in the country outside Superior.

Photo by Alan Miller